Kill Cure

JULIAN RATHBONE

St. Martin's Press/New York

PART I

Claire Mundham

page 7

PART II

Nur, Alp and Mr Mundham

page 51

PART III

Claire Again

page 77

PART IV

The City

page 131

PART I : CLAIRE MUNDHAM

CHAPTER I

It was a good thing, Claire thought, to be in the leading vehicle: from Trieste to Bangladesh with one's view limited by the rear of the Volkswagen van in front would be a bit much, and, already, as the mountain mists round Potojna cleared there were views—albeit of fairly ordinary forest and mountain—that were worth seeing. She smiled happily to herself as the sun flashed through beeches and the road curled above a brown trout stream, and then she glanced, a little shyly, at her companion, Robin Bury. She wondered if he could possibly realize how excited she was, how she could still hardly believe her luck in being chosen as the fifth member of the CHAP expedition to Bangladesh.

Robin certainly sensed something—perhaps just that she had turned slightly towards him. For a second he looked at her before his eyes returned to the road and the back of the large petrol tanker that now loomed up ahead, spewing out black smoke. He wondered, not for the first time, if it really was such a clever idea, having her along with them. He manoeuvred round the tanker, and glanced in the rear-view mirror.

'Problem, driving in convoy,' he said. 'After you've overtaken something as big as that you've got to wait to be sure the others have got round too. Could easily get ten miles ahead and lose them otherwise. Ah, here they come.'

Claire glanced over her shoulder. Here, indeed they came, the two other vans, both bright orange, found for them by CHAP in Trieste, the first driven by Jack Dealer, the second by Doctor Booker Jones with his girl Donna Liss. They were an oddly assorted party, Claire thought, and her mind drifted back to her interview with CHAP only eight days earlier—already it seemed months ago.

'CHAP rqs girl cook etc overland Bangladesh convoy med supplies, Box 4648.' was the advertisement she had answered in the *New Statesman*. A brief correspondence followed, during which she discovered that CHAP stood for 'Christian Help for Asian People', at the end of which she was invited to 3 Queen Charlotte Square for interview.

The interview had not started well. She had been shown by a cleaning lady into a first floor front room furnished with Victorian tat and lined with bookshelves bearing titles like *The Historical Evidence for St Thomas Didymus's Mission to West India, Collected and critically assessed by J. G. de Pyle, D.D.* After a short wait a portly clergyman with egg-stains on his black dicky and a voice that suggested fruitcake had come in. He had introduced himself as the Reverend Frere, known to his friends, he added with a chuckle, as 'Brer Frere'. After a handshake like the brief conjunction of limp lettuce leaves he waved her into a deeply cushioned sofa which left her either sprawled provocatively with her feet off the ground or perched pertly on the edge.

'The others will be here shortly,' he had gone on to say. 'In the meantime perhaps I could tell you a little about CHAP.'

CHAP it appeared had been founded by an American philanthropist and two wealthy widows. Its foundation had left it independent of public support although it was registered as a charity. It existed to give help anywhere in Asia where the Board of Trustees felt it could act usefully.

'I, my dear, I am secretary to the Trustees,' Frere had

concluded. 'Ah, I think I hear them coming. No don't stand up, that sofa is very awkward, I really ought to replace it. Yes, here they are.'

Claire, arrested in her perch, had had to crane round. She felt suddenly overcome with shyness and was conscious of a drop of moisture forming near the end of her nose. To add to her anxiety she was amazed to find that she recognized both of the men who had come in.

'Miss Mundham, may I present Mr Robin Bury and Mr Jack Dealer? I asked Miss Mundham to remain seated. The sofa—so awkward.'

'How do you do?' asked Robin Bury.

'Hi,' said Jack Dealer.

Claire smiled and sniffed.

Jack Dealer sat on the floor with his back to the marble column that supported the fireplace; Robin Bury perched on the creaky arm of the sofa. They were attentive, like men in an ad for rum or vermouth and she had felt a little more at ease, though her heart had continued to pound at the nearness of so much notoriety.

Dealer, longshoreman from San Diego, turned Rock singer, turned revolutionary, was dressed, as he always was on T.V., in soft black leather and jeans. He was, of course, older than she had thought, and his widow's peak more pronounced by the inroads of baldness on either side of it. However, at the back his bleached hair was as long as General Custer's and curled below his shoulders. He was a heavy man, large and very strong looking, almost bullish, but with the pallor of a man who works at night.

Bury was as English as Dealer was transatlantic. He was tall, thin, about thirty, with an ascetic face, which, however, smiled charmingly when he wanted it to. His eyes were large and bright, serious and penetrating. He seemed always in motion, and his hands, with long tapering fingers, flapped and signalled like etiolated wings when he talked. He was dressed in old flannels, sweater and

9

sandals. Claire knew him to have been a lecturer in anthropology who had recently and with more publicity renounced the academic life to play a more active part in the politics of the Left.

They had asked her sensible questions in a business-like way. Jack Dealer posed his with his face turned away from her; he drawled them and then hooked round with his head to hear her answers. Robin was more courteous, but he spoke with a solemnity which seemed to imply that less than honest answers would be a betrayal. Frere said nothing but pretended to be busy behind his desk.

'You have no dependants, people who will be disturbed if you are away for a long time?'

'No.'

'Parents?'

'Mother and father. They're not old. Just sort of middle-aged. They don't need me.'

'Miss Mundham, are you engaged? Do you have a particular boy friend?'

'No.'

'You have had boy friends. I don't mean to pry, but it would be a nuisance if you received a letter saying wedding bells would ring out if only you would return.'

'No, no one like that.'

'Are you fit?'

'Yes.'

'Why do you sniff all the time?'

'I often do if I'm nervous.'

'Have you seen a doctor about it?'

'Yes. He said I would get over it in time.'

'You look rather frail.'

'I travelled for nine months roughing it and I never had more than a cold.' Sniff.

'An everlasting cold.' This came from Robin.

'And I shall not die of it,' said Claire, recognizing the quotation.

'You travelled with a boy?' Dealer's head hooked round.

'Yes. And others.'

'You slept with him?'

'I'm neither a prude nor a lesbian.'

They liked that answer and she could see that they did.

'Nor am I an easy lay,' she added, and was pleased to put them slightly out of countenance. The Reverend Frere had coughed apologetically and she had begun to feel more at ease.

They had asked her why she wanted to go and she had said that she had sympathy for oppressed minorities everywhere and this particularly seemed to please them. They tried too to probe her ability to keep house under primitive conditions, but their questions were superficial, probably, she suspected, out of ignorance.

'Do you belong to any political organization or party?'

'No.'

'Why not?'

'I don't know. Laziness I suppose and there doesn't seem much point. I go to rallies and that if I think they are going to be some use in something important...' It had suddenly seemed silly to say that she had been to the Bangladesh rally four weeks before.

'Union?'

'I'm sorry?'

'Do you belong to a Trade Union?'

'I think I'm a member of NALGO.'

'Think?'

'Well, I joined when I first started work at Heathleigh Borough Library, but that's just about a year ago, and perhaps my subscription has lapsed.'

They had asked her about her passport, and how soon she would be able to go. Then there was a pause and the three men looked at each other. The Reverend Frere rose.

'Miss Mundham, would you care to wait outside for a moment?'

She had gathered up her folk-weave bag and struggled to her feet. Frere had parked her on a high backed chair on the landing in front of a reproduction of Watts' 'Hope'. The blindfold, Claire had thought, made the lady look decidedly vulnerable.

The road, having crossed some watershed in the Julian Alps, began to descend and quite suddenly the morning sun shone brightly and warmly in their faces.

'I should imagine these vans can get quite hot,' Claire volunteered. She still felt quite shy of Robin Bury and she felt a need to pat the black padded dashboard in front of her, almost by way of explanation.

'Let's try the air conditioning.'

She liked the rather boyish smile that went with this. He pulled down a blue lever and a gust of cold air blew into her face.

'Look, you can adjust the vent by turning it round in its socket, and the strength by sliding the button in the middle of it.'

Rather awkwardly she fiddled with the vent, wondering what he was making of her gaucheness with such a simple thing. She sat back and gazed out of her window. Patches of cultivated land bearing maize and vines had taken the place of the forest. A signpost indicated that they were still on the road to Zagreb. Claire's thoughts drifted away again.

After a very short interval, hardly long enough to get out a tissue and deal with her drip, Brer Frere had reappeared and ushered her back in, and, all smiles and congratulations, the three men had offered her a place on the CHAP expedition. The rest of the interview had been practical and the result of it all was that six days later, following their instructions, she had been seen off by her Father at Victoria, changed at Paris, and arrived at Trieste to be met by Bury and Dealer and introduced to the other two members of the expedition—Doctor Booker Jones and Donna Liss.

Booker Jones was black, handsome, animated, and laughed a lot. He was a graduate of Northwestern and had been doing biochemical research in Sweden. Donna obviously adored him and together they made what Claire's mother would have called a striking couple. She had thick hair beautifully cut in half curls that suggested wantonness without being untidy, a full mouth that turned up at the corners, big dark eyes with heavy lids, and a small slightly aquiline nose. Both had been rather expensively if casually dressed and Claire had begun to feel rather self-conscious in the jeans and smock she had chosen to travel in. However, they had been fun, indeed the evening had been fun, and she now rather regretted that they were travelling in separate vehicles, and that for much of the expedition the most she would see of Booker and Donna would be glimpses of their van in the rear-view mirror.

The vans too had been a pleasant surprise. Vaguely Claire had supposed that they would be travelling in some discomfort in jeeps with watercans and spare tyres strapped all round and wire mesh in front of the windscreens. Instead there were these three Volkswagen vans, bought cheaply, it was explained, by CHAP from a party of Australians who had run out of funds. Two of them, the one she shared with Robin and the one Booker and Donna were driving, had been converted, with windows, bunks, 'gaz' burners, into motor caravans. The third remained a van and carried most of their luggage and yet was only half loaded. The space, Dealer explained, was for the medical supplies, which, he said, were still to be picked up.

The first day of the CHAP expedition's journey wore

on pleasantly enough. They stopped at midday at the motel near Brod on the motorway between Zagreb and Belgrade and ate goulash while the heat built up over the plain and maize. Small children from a coachload of workers' families returning from a holiday in Rijeka wrote their names in strange alphabets in the dust that had already collected on the sides of the vans. To the amusement of everyone else Claire burnt her mouth biting unaware on a chili pepper.

In the evening they stopped at the rebuilt hotel at Skopje where they were entertained by a gipsy violinist who played the 'Blue Danube' and a melancholy waiter who spoke English with a marked Kensington accent. Bury explained that they would not be roughing it until they reached Eastern Turkey, and in the meantime, since CHAP was paying, they might as well enjoy themselves.

The waiter cleared away the dishes and brought coffees and slibowicz.

'I worked at the Savoy,' he said. 'Before the war. Do you know the Savoy?'

'Not well,' 'Sure do,' said Bury and Dealer simultaneously.

'I was dropped by parachute in January nineteen forty-four,' said the waiter. 'To meet Marshal Tito and the Partisans. But I never found them.'

Claire noticed that he had lost three fingers from his left hand.

'Before that I worked at the Savoy.'

Dealer gulped down his slibowicz. 'Booker,' he said, 'tell us now how we are going to get these medical supplies.'

The black man pushed back his chair and leaned forward, his long fingers dangling between his knees but flexing up every now and then as he made his points.

'The drug we are taking is Panmycin or...,' and he filled in with a polysyllabic formula. 'You may have read about this in the press. It's a new wide spectrum antibiotic developed in Russia but soon to be manufactured in U.K. and U.S. by the General Drug Company. I have been doing research on it, but the Russians have released only very little and none has yet been synthesized in the West. CHAP had heard of it and they contacted me; I made enquiries and discovered that there was no hope of persuading the Russians to release it in bulk for Bangladesh, but a Russian research doctor I was working with in Sweden told me that there was a stockpile in Bulgaria, and that colleagues of his, humane men, were prepared to smuggle several thousand doses across the border into Greece if we could arrange a rendezvous. It's worth any slight risk for us, because you see Panmycin is effective against Asiatic cholera. So, the day after tomorrow we leave Thessalonika in the late afternoon, arrive near the Bulgarian border three hours before dawn, make our way into the mountains and get the stuff across. No risk for us, but a hell of a risk for the Russian doctor who is going to get it to us. O.K.? Just remember that until Panmycin there was no known cure for cholera, and that cholera is an obscene and agonizing thing that nearly always kills.'

Dealer wiped his mouth on the back of his hand and set down his cup.

'Why,' he drawled, 'don't we get transit visas for Bulgaria, pick up the stuff in Sofia, and cut out the risk for this Russian guy?'

'It wouldn't work,' said Booker. 'The Customs checks on the Bulgarian frontier are very thorough. If they found the Panmycin we should be arrested; it would mean labour camps for Doctor Feyordorivich, and likely death for nine thousand Bengalese who may already be in contact with the cholera salmonella. I wouldn't wish that on anyone.'

'O.K.,' said Jack. 'So we don't go to Sofia.'

Later, in bed that night, Claire could not shake off a disturbed feeling about the whole expedition, a feeling which at times became almost painful. The bed creaked, the room smelt of derris powder or something similar, voices outside called to each other, sometimes raucously, in strange tongues, a child cried and a woman laughed. It was all a long way from the normality of Heathleigh, the London suburb that had always been her home, a long way from the borough library and the tidy housewives and the high school children, a long way from her father and the dahlias he so much cherished and which were just coming to their best. She shifted uneasily in the noisy bed. Bury, she supposed was all right, but there was a nerviness about him that she did not quite like; Dealer frightened her, he seemed such a bull of a man. Booker and Donna were too much in love—they excluded other people, and Booker too was frightening: he had too much energy, and he was touchy too. He could be almost spiteful to Donna. And what a crew they were! What an unlikely combination! And how unlike the group of committed youngsters she had imagined when she had first read the advertisement. And now there was this strange business of smuggling—what was it?—Panmycin. Surely that must be dangerous. She moved again and realized she had almost called aloud for her father.

The returning thought of him was something of a comfort. He had been very good when she had told him about the expedition. As always his refrain had been 'Just as you say, dear,' and he had not made any reference to her last adventure which had ended in Barcelona on a cannabis charge. That had been awful, and the boy she had been with and whose cannabis it was, was still in prison in Spain. But her father had been wonderful, coming out to Spain, seeing the Consul and the Spanish police, and not a word of reproach...

Feeling more secure Claire slept.

16

CHAPTER II

At noon the next day the CHAP expedition crossed into Northern Greece and by late afternoon was established in another hotel at Thessalonika. This hotel, Claire decided, was just right: it fitted the town. Cobbled streets intersected smart boulevards, half-timbered houses were nudged together between concrete blocks, and everything seemed to lead inevitably to the long curving waterfront with its decayed Edwardian hotels, its warehouses, its cafés, and its air of a minor watering place smeared with the oil and grease of a modern port. The hotel was on a corner. The stuccoed but peeling façade faced the sea; the side on which her room was, overlooked a narrow street and an open air cinema. As she lay on the bed in the gathering dusk waiting for the others to call her for dinner raucous music, badly amplified, blared up from below. By standing on tip-toe and craning her head round the slatted shutters she could just get a view of Jean Gabin's head. She identified the film as an old 'roman policier' but so bad was the sound-track that it took her a minute to realize it had been dubbed into Greek.

'Isn't it awful?'

Claire turned and found that Donna had slipped in behind her. The American girl was wearing a brown silk blouse patterned vaguely with orange flowers, and brown cord trousers. Already Claire had learned to marvel at the number of clothes Donna had managed to bring. As usual the dark hair was immaculately wanton and hoops of gold glinted through it.

'Awful?'

'The noise. That damned movie place. Talk about Coca-cola culture—we invent the drive-in and because they have no cars, they turn it into a walk-in. The only difference is that the whole neighbourhood shares the noise.'

'I quite like it.'

'You won't at one o'clock in the morning. They don't close till then.'

'Anyway, I'm sure they had cinemas like this before you had drive-ins.' Claire laughed to defuse the implied snub.

'Maybe. Claire, what do you think of this business tomorrow night?'

'Business? Oh, you mean picking up the ... Panmycin on the Bulgarian border.'

'Yes, just that.'

Donna took a king-size Chesterfield out of its scarlet pack and lit it with a tiny gold lighter. She blew out smoke from pursed lips, crossed her legs, and with a shake of her glorious curls put her elbow on her knee and cupped her chin in her hand. Claire was irresistibly reminded of the heroines of the movies in the forties and fifties whose resurrection on the telly her father welcomed so happily.

'I don't know,' she said. 'I suppose I've tried not to think about it. Does it worry you?'

'It worries me. Oh, I don't mean I couldn't sleep for it, but it worries me. It's so unreal.'

'I suppose this sort of thing always is.'

'I guess so. But it's not just that. They had supplies in Sweden so why do we have to get them smuggled out of Russia or Bulgaria or wherever?'

'But Booker said they had only samples in Sweden. I mean they wouldn't use ten thousand doses for testing.'

'No, that's right, they wouldn't.'

They sat in silence for a moment. A fusillade of shots rang out and police sirens wailed from the cinema.

'It's like we lived in Chicago in prohibition.'

'There must be something else to make you worried.'

'Oh, I don't know. It's just that Booker's been too darned cagey about the whole thing.'

'You don't think it will be dangerous, do you?'

'They said it won't. Anyway they're leaving us safely behind them, so we'll be all right.'

'But perhaps not Booker.'

'Perhaps not.' Donna sighed briefly and stubbed out her cigarette in a glass dish on the varnished dressing table. 'And I expect that's why I'm worried. Come on, let's go down.'

It appeared that the men had decided that they would not eat in the hotel but in a tavern on the front. The short walk seemed magical to Claire. Dull street lights competed with the red velvet sky and lost; the black water was streaked with phosphorescence; everywhere there was twangling music and noise. Street vendors grilled lumps of meat on vertical spits beneath naphtha lamps and a host of strange odours invaded her nostrils: burning meat, spices, the farmyard smells of donkeys and of the mules pulling phaetons, garlic-tainted exhaust fumes, and the pure sharpness of orange trees growing in tubs outside the cafés.

They found the tavern. It was small, low-ceilinged, scruffy, and hazy with smoke, but the food was reasonable. They ate huge prawns with a burning garlic sauce, cold aubergines which had been stewed in oil, and they drank thin resinated wine which had been drawn from a barrel into an uncorked bottle.

They drank too much, and later Jack ordered a bottle of local brandy. When a two piece band came in off the street, he joined them. He strummed ineffectually on the balalaika and then stamped his feet, waving a large red handkerchief. The Greeks cheered obsequiously, but to Claire, struggling a little to reduce two Jack Dealers to one, he appeared a bit ridiculous. In fact, she thought, altogether ridiculous, with his heavy face sweating, his long, thin, receding hair swaying behind his bull neck, and his too tight jeans.

Her vision was not shared by two American soldiers with NATO shoulder flashes, who now drifted in. One of them, a youth with crew-cut, glasses and a stomach that tried to nudge its way through his dun cotton shirt, recognized Jack Dealer and brought his companion over to their table.

'Is that really Jack Dealer?' he asked. 'I mean the real Jack Dealer?'

They told him he was and they exchanged pleasantries but it was obvious that all the Americans were interested in was making actual contact with the folk hero. They did not have to wait long. Jack gave the floor an extra stamp a beat behind the band's final chord, flung his handkerchief in the air, shouted 'olé', and staggered across to them.

'Palefaces from stateside, yippee,' he bellowed, and flung his arms round their shoulders, collapsing forward with mock drunkenness between them. Booker pushed a chair in behind and the folk hero fell into it. Fervent introductions and strong masculine handgrips were exchanged.

'Well fellas, how long you been here?' demanded Jack. '... and what's it like over here? What's the food like? All "made in U.S.A.", right? Even the water I guess, flown out from our own polluted lakes, eh? Nothing personal, soldier, you know how I feel about this kind of thing, it's all in my songs. But they feed you all right, huh? Home cooking, five days a week, and they fly you in filet mignon and French fries from Paris on weekends, right?' They laughed and blushed and laughed again as he cajoled them, flattered them, insulted them, and made it up again.

Claire had to admire the performance—the ageing animal trainer with sedated beasts whose teeth had been drawn. 'And do they keep you busy here, or are you just sitting around on your asses enjoying a European tour at Uncle Sam's expense?'

'Oh no, Jack, don't get us wrong,' the bespectacled lieutenant was suddenly serious. 'The work we're doing here is vital to national security and there's plenty to be done. You have no idea what problems these Greeks have and over the border...'

'Hold it,' cried Jack. 'Hold it right there. One more word and there'll be another leak for the Pentagon to explain. Remember, "Loose lips sink ships",' he orated with false solemnity. 'No my friend, we believe you, say no more, we understand. For you it's combat ready, all the way.'

'Yes, Jack,' said the lieutenant, still so earnest that his glass shook a little, 'it really is all the way.'

Not much later Jack eased the American soldiers to the door and with much more shouting and waving, saw them down the street. He returned to the table looking tired, rather more obviously middle-aged than usual, and sober too.

'Sorry about that. My public, I guess. I can't stop myself, and my agent does say that it helps record sales.' He looked up, his eyes bleary and bloodshot. His huge palm swung across the table in a mock Hollywood gesture as if to sweep the glasses and bottles to the floor. 'Let's get out of here. It's a shit hole. Don't know why we came.'

And stumbling a little he led them out into the cool street.

CHAPTER III

It was, thought Claire, surprisingly cold, and a bit frightening, sitting in a Volkswagen van on a moonless night, at the end of a stony track, not more than a mile, she supposed, from the Iron Curtain. The dull glow from the parking lights lit up a crude road barrier; half an hour earlier Robin, Jack and Booker had hoisted themselves over the low boom and disappeared into the darkness beyond. Now there were only indistinct mountains, almost bare of vegetation it seemed, and the unsympathetic glory of the Milky Way in a black sky.

Donna stirred in the passenger seat beside her and shook out her third Chesterfield. The little gold lighter blazed and reduced the already indistinct rocks to nothingness. The cigarette smoke was cold and acrid and Claire felt a headache beginning to throb across her forehead.

'What's the time?' she asked.

Donna held her wrist in the glow from the dashboard and peered at her tiny gold wristwatch.

'Just after three. Twenty minutes before we can expect them. An hour, they said, before we need worry.'

She smoked hard for a minute or two and then went on with a shake of her luxurious hair. 'This is goddam ridiculous. Not worry? What the hell do they think we are?'

Claire glanced at her. The American girl was biting on her full bottom lip and staring at her hands from eyes that looked moist.

'I'm sure they'll be all right.'

'How can you say that? There must be a risk. There has to be. You don't smuggle stuff out of countries like Bulgaria without a risk. Especially at night on wild stretches of frontier like this. At least at an official crossing point they'd ask questions before shooting. Here I suppose the patrols just shoot. It's all so damned ridiculous.'

Claire sat in silence for a bit and then, as slyly as she could manage it, wound down the window.

'I thought you were cold.' Donna wriggled more deeply into the sheepskin jacket she was wearing.

'Where did you meet Booker?' Claire asked, hoping to distract her companion's attention.

'At a party. In New York. It was a hell of a party. All "radical chic", you know? Bernstein was there, even. Booker was one of the exhibits—black man who made good, top biochemist, and all that. They had a good "Soul" band.'

'Really?'

'Yeah, really. He danced with me. It was the first time I really knew I had a body.'

Claire thought of the litheness of the black man, his easy, lazy movements, and the hard spareness of his frame.

'What were you doing in New York?'

'Then? I was teaching. Special tutoring for backward readers in the ghettos. Joke. They're all backward readers there. Christ, what was that?'

'What?'

'Listen. Again.'

Muffled by distance, no less innocuous than a child cracking a whip, two tiny concussions.

'Gunshots, three at least.'

'How do you know? It could have been a lorry backfiring down on the main road.' But Claire could feel her scalp prickling.

'Ten miles away? Hush.'

23

They held their breaths and in the stillness Claire could hear her heart beating.

'I know gunshots,' Donna whispered. 'I've seen and heard shots fired in streets, in broad daylight. Oh hell, I hate it. I hate it all.'

Claire put her hand on Donna's and felt it tremble. She wondered if she knew the girl well enough to put an arm round her shoulder. She felt suddenly lonely, insecure rather than frightened. It was all so strange, so beyond her experience, she did not know what to do.

'They'll be all right,' she murmured.

Donna glared at her, almost angry, and then shrugged and sighed.

Time passed.

'I want to get out, I can't stand this. I'm going out.'

'There's ten minutes yet. They can't be any quicker. Not with things to carry in the dark.'

Donna glanced at her watch.

'Five minutes, then I'm going.'

Running, pounding footsteps.

'Put the headlights on,' cried Donna, and launched herself out of the van.

Into the glare stumbled Robin. His shirt was torn, his face white and smeared with blood.

'They shot at us,' he gasped. 'Someone shot at us. At the border. Booker was hit.'

'Oh Jesus Christ!'

'It's all right. Just a graze on his arm. It's very clean, but it's bleeding a bit.' He had got round to the back of the van and was throwing blankets and clothes out on to the ground. 'Where the hell is the first aid kit? He's all right, I promise you, but he could use a bandage. Here it is. He's only half a mile away, and there's no question of the Bulgarians crossing the border after us.

'I'm coming with you,' said Donna.

'No, stay here.'

24

'I'm coming with you.'

'I'm not staying here on my own,' said Claire.

Robin hesitated, looking at each girl in turn.

'All right. I suppose this lot will be safe for half an hour. It'll have to be. You can see Booker back here while I help Jack with the boxes. Bring a torch. I warn you, it's rough going in the dark.'

Donna struggled after Robin over the pole and he gave her a hand as both her legs swung off the ground. Claire, left with the torch in her hand, hesitated and then ducked under. The track climbed quickly and soon became almost indistinct amongst boulders and debris; only white stones set at twenty yard intervals showed that they were still on the right path. Donna and Robin remained ahead, as far as the glow of Claire's torch would allow them, and she hobbled behind with a badly barked shin. Between grunts and gasps she could hear them talking, and occasionally could see Robin's hand flung out to steady the American girl.

'How much further?'

'Not more than a quarter of a mile, but it'll seem further.'

'What happened?'

'We came to a cairn. Jack said it marked the beginning of No-Man's land, the three hundred metre strip on either side of the actual border. He and Booker went on. I couldn't see them. They came back with two cases and went for the third. They'd only been gone five minutes this time when the shooting started. They came back, Booker with his arm hurt and Jack carrying the third case.'

'Are you all right?' called Claire, running a step or so to catch up. After all there had been blood on him too.

'Yes. I fell coming down. That's all.'

Suddenly another shot cracked out. There was no flash that they could see, but the report seemed near and it echoed briefly.

'For Christ's sake, put the flashlight out.' The voice, Jack's, seemed even closer.

Claire felt sick with fear as she rammed the torch, lens down, into the ground, and groped at the switch. She had been shot at. Someone up there had shot at the light— the light she was carrying. A great sob—misery, fear, loneliness—struggled out of her throat.

'Over here. It's all right. This way. We're to your left. They won't cross the border and they won't shoot again, not without anything to shoot at. Even if they do, it would be a miracle if they got near us.'

A red glow, the tip of a cigarette, blossomed ahead and to the left, about twenty yards away, and behind it Claire could just identify Jack's face. A pyramid of stones rose behind him. Half crawling, half running, bent double, she followed the other two into its shelter.

'All right. Put the light on again. We're safe behind this.'

For a moment Claire thought she had broken it but she gave it a shake and it came on again. Jack was on his haunches, the cigarette dangling between his large fingers; to his right lay Booker, his teeth grinning whitely; between them three boxes, each about the size of a cabin trunk, lay where they had been dropped. The black man was clutching a wad of stuff—a handkerchief perhaps—to his left arm, and blood oozed darkly between his fingers.

Robin fumbled at the first aid box and then prised the sticky fingers and the dressing away. Claire caught a brief glimpse of a long gash gaping across the arm—the inside lips of the wound looked grey—and then she turned away. Donna took the torch out of her hand.

'It needs stitches,' Robin muttered.

'Man, I know that. Can you put them in?'

'I never have, but you tell me what to do and I'll have a go.'

'Right. First, novocaine, aerosol. Then disinfectant.

Thread the needle. O.K. Steady now. About an eighth of an inch out from the wound. No, go at it from the other side. Oooch, Goddamn you, you pink bastard. No, don't mind me, you're doing fine. Donna, another squirt with that aerosol. No, really Robin you're doing fine. Make a doctor of you yet. O.K., now knot it. Christ, don't worry about what knot, gently, don't tear it. Good man. Three more like that should do it...'

Claire crept away towards Jack. To her surprise he put his huge arm round her, folding her inside his fleece-lined coat, which had been draped round his shoulders.

'Cigarette?'

'No thanks.' She sniffed and felt her eyes pricking. There was an odd smell about him.

'Handkerchief?'

'Thanks.' She took it and blew, annoyed that after four days her complaint had started up again. Booker had given her pills for it, but they were down in the car.

'That shot sounded awfully close,' she murmured.

'Not really. Two hundred yards, maybe three. We're in the end of a valley, you know. The reverberations made it sound closer.'

'And they really won't come nearer?'

'Not them. They don't know who we've got here. Might have half the Greek army for all they know.'

Although Dealer frightened her he was warm and Claire felt comforted, but she went on sniffing.

Ten minutes or so later Robin and the girls helped Booker back down the path, leaving Jack at the cairn. Then Robin returned to help him with the cases. It was over an hour before they were all safely back. They decided to stay in the vans until daylight. They drank some of Jack's whisky and tried to sleep. Claire brooded. Robin was close enough for her to feel his leg against hers, but as the awareness of it crossed her mind, he shifted awkwardly away in the darkness. It was ridiculous. Jack had so easily put his arm around her. She remembered the smell of the American's hand, almost felt its weight again. Tangy, masculine, tobacco, machine oil, and a hint of some other evocative odour. Bonfires. Guy Fawkes. She dozed. Why couldn't Robin give her that much comfort? Hell. She shifted away and bunched her coat into a pillow and dozed again.

Dawn. Stars paling. She shivered and let herself out. Donna appeared and together they set about making coffee while the pearly light spread over the hills around them. There was a heavy dew on the cars and the air was almost icy. They didn't speak, not even when Claire splashed water on Donna's wrist as they tried clumsily to fill the kettle. Donna looked grey, and, for once, dishevelled. They carried the coffee in to the men, and, with the warmth of it, began to feel a little better. The sun lifted above a crag.

Booker pulled himself out awkwardly, stretched one arm, and yawned noisily, a basso profundo of a yawn.

'White girl,' he rumbled, 'you fix me some bacon 'n eggs, good and quick now y'hear?'

Donna turned to reach out the cooking things, and Booker slapped her behind with his good hand.

'Yo keep yo han' to yoself, yo no-good niggrah,' she cried, and they all laughed.

CHAPTER IV

At Alexandropolis, the last town in Greece, Claire had her photograph taken in her underwear.

They had parked the vans near the small square and Booker and Jack had gone off to find a doctor who would dress Booker's arm properly leaving the other three drinking mineral water and thick coffee. Claire soon felt bored since neither Donna nor Robin had much to say and after a time she wandered off down the narrow streets. She felt exhausted and listless after the sleepless and frightening night, and irritated that Robin had stayed at the café with Donna.

She found her way out of the town and on to a small beach. There were bathing huts on dunes in front of a little pine wood which screened the beach from the road, but the huts were locked up and no-one seemed to be about. She sat for five minutes on gritty sand—it was more a fine shingle—and gazed at the calm spread of the sea. At first the gentle lapping, the slow rush and fall, were enough to soothe her as she picked over the whitened sea-wrack, but soon she became aware again of the flaky dryness that seemed to have infected her armpits, and the soreness of her nose and eyes. The temptation to swim became irresistible.

Her pants and bra were jersey knit stretch nylon and not fancy—they would pass she felt sure for a bikini. She would chance the effect of water on their opaqueness, and before doubts could become fears, she had lifted off her smock, wriggled out of her jeans, and scampered into the sea. She had to wade some distance before the bottom shelved, but the water was not cold. She scooped up handfuls and kicked and pranced, sending drops of gold into the morning air around her. At last she could launch herself forward to swim steadily out to sea. She turned on her back, and spread her arms, shutting her eyes against the sun. Relaxed completely she lay on the sea almost sleeping, savouring the restfulness of it all. In just over a year she had forgotten the delight of swimming in warm buoyant waters.

The others. It would not do to keep them waiting. She rolled over and turned for the shore, surprised to see how far it was, and then almost swallowed water. There was a strange man standing beside her clothes. She felt for the bottom, swam on, found it, stood, and looked down at her chest. It would not do. She looked like something on the cover of a girlie magazine. At school it had been a trick of hers when embarrassed to compose imaginary letters to Evelyn Home and then the answer. Dear Evelyn Home ... Dear 'Covered in Confusion', Just walk out of the sea as if nothing was wrong, pull on your clothes, and stroll away. The chances are that nothing will happen, he'll just look at you, and you'll never see him again. Right. Really, it was quite funny. As she splashed nearer she could see that he was quite young, thin moustache, dark suit, black tie. Not a likely looking rapist. But ... he had a camera. What should she do? Strike a coy pose, smile provocatively? Thin-lipped and looking determinedly over his left shoulder she strode up the shingle. The shutter clicked, the man turned sharply and walked away into the pines.

Half an hour later they were on the road again. Robin and Claire led the way, Jack followed with the cases of Panmycin, Donna and Booker last with Donna driving since

Booker now had his arm in a sling. They passed a deserted village with a broken minaret rising above fallen roofs and overgrown gardens.

'That's the second village like that we've seen today. It's almost as if there had been a plague,' Claire remarked.

'Moslems lived here until recently,' said Robin. 'They were resettled across the border during the last confrontation over Cyprus in the late sixties. There was nearly a war and the Greeks burned their crops. Did you enjoy your swim?'

'Very much. I feel much better for it. It really was lovely, although an idiot man nearly spoiled it.'

'What idiot man?'

In the rush to get going again—they had been waiting for her—she had not mentioned the incident.

'When I came out there was this man standing by my things. He took a photograph of me as I got near him and then he walked away.'

Robin was silent for a moment, staring down the straight white road which stretched between fields of corn.

'What was he like?' he asked.

'Young, well-dressed. Not the snooping type I should have thought.'

'He sounds like the man who came and took pictures of us at the café. He left a card—it's under the dashboard.'

Claire fumbled in the rubbish that had already accumulated and found a slip of pasteboard with an Alexandropolis address typed on it.

'He didn't look like a beach photographer,' she said.

'No, I suppose not. And he didn't leave you a card?'

'No.' Her mind went back to the horror of the night before. 'Do you think it had anything to do with last night?'

'I don't see how it could. Anyway, what does it matter? We've got the Panmycin, and it doesn't bother me to think the man was a Bulgarian agent and that our pictures are now in the K.G.B.'s files.'

Claire shuddered.

'Are you cold? Your underthings must be damp.'

'No. Yes. Yes, I suppose I am.'

'Well you'll be able to change at the frontier. Only ten minutes or so now.'

The Greek frontier post was set in an airy copse of poplars whose leaves were just beginning to turn: the blue and white flag fluttered gently amongst the green and gold. There were striped barriers, prohibitory notices in four languages, and men in at least three different kinds of uniform. Beyond the complex of low, white buildings a steel girder bridge spanned a wide, slow river.

'Shall I change here or wait till we've crossed?' asked Claire.

'I should change here. We're bound to be some time.'

As the officials closed in on the three vehicles she slipped away to a shed-like building set apart from the rest—men at one end, women at the other. Inside it was dark, damp and smelly, there were six cubicles—the floor of the first was flooded, the second less so, and the last dry enough for her to change without trailing any of her garments in the puddles. Large mosquitoes hung in the air at head height and the cracked W.C. pedestal did not bear looking into. Just as she was adjusting her beads she was startled to hear male voices, very close, and then she realized that they were coming through a ventilator grille high up near the ceiling in the rough-cast thin partition wall. Nevertheless she could make out only what one of the two men was saying.

'It went O.K. then?'

A grunt.

'You got them down the hill in the dark?'

Another grunt.

'Did you try either of the deception plans? ... Yep, I think that was the better one. You suppose it worked?'

The other man started to speak clearly and Claire heard three words.

'Arnold, I'm not...,' then all was lost in a sudden rush of water as the urinals on the other side of the wall all flushed together.

Claire waited for the noise to subside. She felt sure that what she had heard related to the Panmycin. What else could have been 'got down the hill in the dark'? What else was there? Already she was forgetting the exact wording—something about a plan? And deception—that was it. Who had been deceived?

The rush of running water stopped, but the men had gone. Claire went out, blinking, into the hot, dusty sunlight, but still she shivered and there were goosepimples on her arms. She wandered through a car-park, trying to make sense of what she had heard.

'Not this way, ma'am, the public sector is back over there.' Claire absently acknowledged the G.I. who leant against the bonnet of a NATO jeep, and retraced her footsteps. The G.I. had fixed in her mind that at least one of the voices she had heard was American.

'Claire, Claire.'

Through a gap in the trees and buildings she could see Robin on the roadside about a hundred yards away. He turned and saw her.

'Come on, Claire. They've cleared us and we must go on.'

The sight of him, so tall, so very British, was reassuring, and she broke into a trot to catch him. She wanted to talk to him, tell him about what she had heard, and be told there was nothing to worry about. Then her stride faltered as she considered. If the conversation had been about their adventure and the Panmycin, then the other voice had to be Jack, Booker, or ... Robin. Which? What had the other voice said? 'Arnold, I'm not...'? that was absurd. She tried to make the words sound in her head. Had there been an accent, an American one? She couldn't be sure. But one thing she did feel certain about was that she did not want whomever she had heard to know that she had been eavesdropping. And it just could have been Robin.

She came on to the road and saw that their convoy was past the first barrier and the second was already raised to let them through. She broke into a run.

Robin started the engine as she climbed in.

'You've been a long time,' he said. Did he sound suspicious? Certainly irritated.

'I'm sorry. I just wanted to stretch my legs.'

The barrier dropped behind them.

CHAPTER V

Rivers make good frontiers and the Maritsa is no exception. Wide, brown and slow it is unavoidable: the first obstacle against the Ottoman invasions of Europe, their last defence when their empire had crumbled; and two thousand years before the Turks Xerxes had reviewed his army on its banks before launching his hordes into Greece, to Thermopylae, Salamis, and Plataea.

'This bridge is very new,' said Robin. 'Ten years ago, we should have had to go all the way up to Edirne and back. Neither side liked the idea of a bridge here—it brings bad neighbours too close. But commerce and tourism triumphed in the end.'

He would have gone on with his lecture, but the bridge, imposing though it was, was not that long.

More barriers, low buildings, poplars—but different uniforms and a red flag with a white crescent and star. Again they got out of the Volkswagen and the police nosed around them, lifting cushions, opening the cupboard at the back, even unscrewing one of the plastic water containers and sniffing at it. Claire looked at them curiously—Turks, not at all dark as she had imagined, indeed paler in a sallow sort of way than the Greeks they had just left. They were courteous too, almost 'galant'. One of them, on lifting a seat and finding her pants neatly folded on top of a pile of clothes, quickly closed it again and turned away with something like a blush.

They moved on to Dealer's van and almost immediately

there was trouble. The two uniformed men had opened the sliding door of the van and lifted one of the cases of Panmycin out on to the ground. Jack intervened at once, first obstructing the customs officer, then speaking loudly and repetitively in the sort of tone angry people adopt with small children or foreigners. Finally he sat on the case and firmly refused to move.

'Hey, Bury, Jones,' he called, 'tell this guy we don't want to open the cases. Tell him what's in them, where we're going, whatever you like, but tell him to leave them alone.'

Robin pushed past the officers leaving Claire on the outside of what was becoming something of a crowd as other people, both travellers and officials, drifted nearer; but she could see Dealer clearly: his face was red, his knees were spread out and his heavy hands firmly planted on them. He was looking up, his head swinging belligerently from face to face above him. He would have looked comic, especially as he was perched so low, had there not been a hint of animal anger in his eyes, mixed, Claire realized, with fear, real fear. But before these impressions could sink in, the group parted and fell silent.

A small, elderly man in a shabby grey suit had joined them. He had greyish, rather oily lank hair and spectacles, and an untidy moustache stained with nicotine. Yet he also had authority. He spoke in English with firm courtesy.

'One moment please. Please to be very quiet.' He snapped his fingers and said something in Turkish. With the speed of a conjuror's sleight of hand one of the uniformed men produced the expedition's passports. The man in the grey suit flipped through them, glancing at each of the party in turn. Claire noticed that his expressionless eyes were a hard blue behind the spectacles.

'I am in charge here. I should like you to come to my office.'

36

Without waiting for an answer he led them across the bright dusty compound into a cool dim room. There were battered filing cabinets against the walls and a large desk untidily strewn with grey papers. A huge fan circled slowly above them. They stood meekly in front of the desk and waited for him to sit down.

'I am the chief customs officer here,' he repeated, 'and I have the authority to send you back to Greece if there is any difficulty. Now,' he picked up one of the papers in front of him and peered at it, 'you are taking medical supplies to East Pakistan. Good, a work of charity. All good Moslems will applaud, even though some of us might feel that you are bringing succour to rebels. What is the nature of these supplies?'

Booker spoke up. 'Panmycin. A new antibiotic, effective, among other things, against Asiatic cholera. Only the Russians have it in bulk, and we procured this shipment from a Russian source.'

'And why is it so important that I should not be allowed to check the cases? They are heavy. They could contain arms, explosives, plastique; I am sorry to say there is a market for such things in Turkey.' His voice became peremptory. 'I must insist. Now, who has the keys?'

There was a moment's awkward silence and two flies buzzed together at the window. Bury cleared his throat.

'Come on Jack,' he said, 'you've got the keys.'

Dealer's eyes narrowed and he swung his head round to Booker.

Booker shrugged. 'Do what the man says.'

Slowly Jack pulled a key ring from his pocket and dropped it on the desk; then he turned on his heel and pushed out past the guards.

Outside the other two cases were dragged out on to the ground and all in turn were opened. Each case contained five trays stacked on top of each other and each tray was filled with small glass phials wrapped in blue tissue paper.

The officer unwrapped one phial, held it up to the light and shook it. It appeared to be half filled with a white crystalline powder, sealed in with a rubber cap. Booker pushed up to him, wincing as his wounded arm nudged past one of the guards.

'It's administered by injection. The bottle is filled with distilled water, the powder dissolved and drawn off into the syringe,' he said.

The man in the grey suit looked at him hard. 'Like heroin,' he said, 'or morphine.'

'For Christ's sake,' cried Booker. 'Do you honestly think we would attempt to smuggle hard drugs in such an obvious way?'

The chief shrugged and spoke rapidly to the uniformed men who began to collect one phial from each tray. Dealer moved forward with such suddenness that one of the uniformed men had to seize his elbow and hold him back. Claire's stomach went cold as she saw the hand of the other guard fumbling at the white plastic gun holster at his belt.

'What the hell are you doing now?' shouted Dealer.

'We are going to retain samples for analysis.'

'But that may take days.'

'You will not be delayed. It will take you at least four days, perhaps five, to cross our country. If the analysis discovers anything unusual we shall be able to find you. In any case you will no doubt stay in Istanbul for a day or two—it is too touristical to rush through. And I assume you are tourists as well as bringers of mercy.' A touch of irony coloured the dry voice. 'We have many such expeditions. We still get young men and women from your countries bringing tents and so on to assist the victims of our last earthquake, although everyone was rehoused before winter came.'

'Look,' Jack was almost out of control. 'You are taking fifteen doses. That could mean the lives of fifteen children.

It's bastards like you, pigs, who have gotten this world into the mess it's in...'

'Mr Dealer. You have committed an offence.' The voice was sour now, caustic even. 'I could arrest you. I could turn you back for what you have said. Get that stuff back in your vehicles and drive on quickly. And during your transit across my country insult no more Turks, and especially do not call Moslems pigs.'

The keys fell in the dust at Dealer's feet. White-faced, the chief of customs turned on his heel and strode away.

Four long days coupled with the tensions of the previous twenty hours or so probably combined to make Claire and Robin edgy towards each other. It was difficult too to be in such close contact with a not unattractive man for so long on terms which seemed to exclude any intimacy closer than a Boy Scoutish chumminess.

'I suppose,' said Claire, as they drove away from the frontier post, 'that that was the frontier in "Topkapi".'

'Eh?' said Robert.

'You know, the film. With Melina Mercouri, Peter Ustinov, Akim Tamiroff, and Robert ...'

'I thought Topkapi was the Ottoman palace in Istanbul.'

'It was a jolly good film. Whenever I think of Istanbul, that's what I think of.'

'I shouldn't think it will be much like the film.'

'Why not?'

'Well, you know, they always romanticize places in that sort of film.'

'What sort of film? How do you know what it was like if you never saw it? It was based on a book by Eric Ambler.'

'Who?'

'Eric Ambler.'

'I'm afraid I don't have much time for novels. I used to like Conrad though.'

'And I like Jane Austen.'

Robin drove on dourly for an hour or so through gently undulating country, not unlike the Wiltshire Downs, but hot and dusty. The day wore on and the sun circled round behind them. Claire felt empty.

'It must be quite late,' she said. 'Can't we stop at the next town for a snack?'

Robin glanced at a signpost. 'There's a place called Tekirdağ in about five minutes. We could stretch our legs. I'll pull in and ask the others.'

He flagged the convoy down and almost before he had pulled on the handbrake Jack was at his window. The American's face looked purple framed in his yellow, lank hair.

'For Christ's sake, why have we stopped?' he bellowed.

'Claire's hungry,' said Robin mildly. 'We could stop at Tekirdağ.'

'Look,' said Jack, 'it's essential we get to Istanbul as soon as we can.'

'I don't see ten minutes is going to make much difference. We'll need petrol before we get there, so we might as well stop now.'

Jack thumped his huge fist on to the door, so hard that Claire half expected there to be a dent. 'We'll use the reserve cans.'

'No, we won't,' said Donna, who had joined them. 'I'm not used to driving such distances without a break. We'll stop at Tekirdağ. Anyway, I shall,' she added with a firm nod of her regroomed hair.

Jack rubbed his lined eyes with his palms drawing the skin lugubriously down his face. He shook his head. 'Very well. Ten minutes while we fill up and the girls can powder their tails or whatever.'

'I want to eat,' wailed Claire.

'Goddamn it,' shouted Jack, and he stamped back to his van.

After their stop they saw the sea and for most of the rest of the way it remained to be glimpsed or scanned to their right. Beaches, villas, villages became more frequent; tiny resorts, marinas, billboards advertising 'otelis' and 'gazinos' crowded closer, and always beyond lay the calm blueness of the Marmora.

Ahead an airliner banked in the golden afternoon light, its wings like quicksilver against the fathomless blue. The road broadened into a motorway and they sped faster down it, three gaudy arrows shot from the sun behind them. A Roman aqueduct kept pace, limped over a broken arch, and subsided. Then, quite suddenly, above trees and shanties, a long line of brown, ochre, red and gold towers and battlements rose in front of them, stretching, it seemed, for miles across their path. The wall was huge, a chain of castles, slashed by the purple shadows of evening, and beyond floated domes and minarets.

'Golly,' said Claire.

'Yes,' said Robin, and negotiating a roundabout he led them through the Topkapi gate into Istanbul.

CHAPTER VI

As passenger in the leading car it was Claire who had to make sense of the street map on her knee, to match it with the bewildering chaos that closed in on them, roaring howling and shrieking from every side: there were taxis that looked as if they had been shot up, and tramcars, lorries, donkeys, cars, suicidal pedestrians; police, high in white pulpits blew whistles at her; taxi drivers screamed oaths; pedestrians walked in front of them and, as they jolted to a stop, looked up blankly and shrugged fatalistically at the foolishness of foreigners. What with all this and streets that turned out unexpectedly to be one way or deadends, steep cobbled hills on which spavined horses slithered and even fell, and finally an old porter carrying a piano on his back who waited till the lights turned green before walking off the kerb, Claire had no time to take in the domes and gardens, the minarets and palaces that floated peacefully always above them and always at the ends of long streets that climbed to the skyline.

At last they dropped to a sheet of grey filthy water crowded with tarry caïques, skiffs, and oily black barges between two long, low, ugly bridges.

'The Golden Horn!' shouted Robin, as they pushed their way across, bumper to bumper, through thousands of commuters who surged off the footwalks.

'Oh no,' cried Claire, but she managed to glance up through the fumes and smoke at the magical skyline behind them, silhouetted against the deepening blue of the sky.

Then they were climbing again through an area which seemed newer, but yet more drab, unrelieved by glimpses of an older, nobler architecture. At last, near the crown of the hill, they found the Galata Palas Oteli.

CHAP had made reservations for them though it hardly seemed necessary. The hotel appeared to be almost empty, the hall a brown barn floored with a marble from which the shine had gone. It was dimly lit by yellow bulbs in ornate brackets which contributed to the overall effect of a fading Edwardian dream of vanished oriental splendour. But Claire's room was comfortable: it had a huge brass bed, an enormous carved wardrobe, and a chipped private bath on claw legs fitted with brass taps and a shower from which the chrome had peeled. She took aspirin and the pills Booker had given her and subsided with relief into the engulfing down mattress.

After an hour or so asleep she bathed and changed, and after losing herself in the dark corridors of the hotel trying to find the staircase—the lift, old, caged, and unmanned, seemed far too dangerous—found that she was the last to join the group. A stranger had joined the party—a short, tubby man in a not too clean suit, swarthy and very hairy. Robin introduced him.

'This is Sami bey. A friend of a friend. Actually he was a student of a friend of mine who taught here for a year. Sami is going to take us later to a discothèque on the Asian side.'

'How do you do?' said Sami, and offered a moist hand. He sat next to Claire at dinner and made her feel, as she put it to herself, 'leant upon'. She feared that she would be expected to dance with him all evening.

'Robin bey's colleague, Doctor Atkinson, was a great man,' he said as he sucked soup. 'But he was a committed structuralist, and when the army took over the government it was certain that his contract would not be renewed.'

'The army took over?' asked Donna.

'Yes ma'am.' Sami's English tended to reflect the origins of whomever had been the last to speak. 'The Turkish Liberation Army and similar groups had gotten out of hand. The two main parties, the Justice Party and the Republican Party, neither of which had an overall majority, could not agree on how to suppress them, there were economic problems too, and so the Army stepped in again.'

'Again?'

'They did before. In 1960. But this last time they did not actually take over the government in an armed coup, they simply set up a coalition with a new Prime Minister—a business man's government of the moderate right, and told them to get on with it. It was less obvious than a coup and probably just as effective.'

'Friend Sami, this disco, this nightclub,' called Dealer, 'is it going to be any good? What about belly-dancers? Ya-ta-ta-a-a-a,' he sang, undulating his rounded mid-riff beneath his tightly stretched shirt. 'Oriental delights in the city of a thousand harems.'

'No, no, nothing of the kind.' Sami turned to Claire. 'There are no dancing girls of the sort Mr Dealer adumbrated. Places such as he described are for tourists. The Red Pasha Club is very modern, very chic. I am sure that ladies like you will find yourselves at home there and there will be nothing distasteful.'

Claire gave him a smile, and repressed the desire to say that she had not travelled two thousand miles to feel at home.

The Red Pasha Club was indeed a drag, though the drive to it was exciting enough. The taxi dropped down steep streets to the quayside, and after a short wait drove on to the ferry. Behind them the Dolmabahce, the last great palace of the Sultans, glowed luminously white above the purple water, a slab of crystalline icing with its perfect rococo mosque at one end and the Hilton, a pillar of light above it. To their right the water in the mouth of the Golden Horn heaved oilily beneath the sharp silhouettes of palaces and mosques, and in front Asia glittered above the Bosphorus, a chain of diamonds on a negress's neck. They passed Leander's Tower, an unauthentic, modern looking block that served as a lighthouse, but the setting was such that Claire decided to accept it and imagined the white arm of Lord Byron curved above the choppy black waves.

Asia turned out to be much like Europe. Near the quay there was a typically harbourish quarter of railway lines, warehouses, and office blocks merging into run-down streets and cafés and small shops, with an atmosphere, thought Claire, not unlike the seedier areas of Southampton or Tilbury. This gave way to a residential area of small apartment blocks occasionally set in tiny gardens. They caught a glimpse of the sea again and then drew into the kerb in front of a building just like the others except that there was a canopy over the door and red neon flashed the message 'Kizil Paşa Kulupisi' and 'Disko'.

Inevitably the club was in the basement, a large room the walls of which had been covered garishly with the heroes of American comics painted crude and large: Batman, Superman, and Charlie Brown rubbed shoulders with more recent arrivals in the pantheon—enormously busted heroines in uniforms that crossed the bunny-girl with the stormtrooper. Coloured lights whirled, and a strobe pulsed above elaborate stereo equipment behind which sat a white-jacketed epicene in a green wig.

'Good, yes,' shouted Sami.

No answer was possible—the noise was shattering.

It was crowded too, but seats had been kept for them

45

in a line against the wall which meant they could not sit facing each other. Sami found bottles of near-Coke garnished with straws and thrust them into their hands. As her eyes grew accustomed to the frenetic flashing Claire noticed one surprising thing—in the crowd of mouthing, strutting, shuddering dancers boys outnumbered girls by nearly two to one; moreover many of them were dancing in front of each other. She wondered if the Red Pasha was gay, but she remembered that she was in a Moslem country and she decided that if these boys were homosexual they were so 'faute de mieux': their sisters were still firmly locked away.

Sami asked her to dance and with a good grace she followed him into the mêlée. To her surprise he danced well with fluid movements in spite of his chunky build and with rather more attention to her own gyrations than she was accustomed to get in England, but the constant pummelling from all sides and the foreign odours of garlic and oil diluted any mild pleasure she might have had. Soon she led Sami firmly back to the chairs.

The disc jockey announced a Soul record and Booker and Donna got up to dance. Perhaps because of his size or because of his blackness they seemed to find room to dance properly. Donna was dressed in her long tasselled skirt. Her sandalled feet shifted and peeped beneath it in delicately taken steps that somehow recalled the real Arabian Nights; her arms turned sinuously in front of her undulating body; her head moved rhythmically back and forward on her long neck; and her hair swayed in syncopation. Her eyes glittered and the corners of her mouth turned up in a smile that was at the same time frozen in conventional ecstasy and yet maintained an expression of amused self awareness, almost ironic in acceptance of her own beauty and that of her man.

But Booker was incapable of framing her, of being her foil. He slouched and padded, unrolled his limbs in the lazy movements of a loping cat, stretched up to concentrate all his power into his centre and then turned suddenly as if to pounce as Donna swirled round him. His hands— pale palms, long fingers spread—caressed the space she had left and the whites of his eyes rolled in mock surrender; his deep voice bayed the lyric, decorating it with his own riffs and grace notes.

When the record finished Claire irreverently recalled the Presley films of her early adolescence. At about this point, she thought, the rich impresario should come in and offer Booker a huge recording contract. She also wondered that his arm had healed so quickly.

No impresario came, but for a moment she thought one had. A door behind the disc jockey's green wig swung back leaving a rectangle of startling blackness. Into it stepped a ghost—the ghost of Che Guevara: beret, dark glasses, beard, olive green battledress, red bandanna, the lot. The absurd disc jockey became aware of the attention focused two feet behind him, turned and lifted the stylus from the record, and flicked a couple of switches. The lights froze.

'Jeee-ss-us,' sighed Donna.

The shadow of a smile crossed the ghost's lips and he raised a hand in a smooth, open-palmed arc—half welcome, half the wave that gracious royalty bestows on loyal subjects. Then the spell broke. The figure murmured to the disc jockey, and swung briskly round the electronic console and into the room. Before he reached them the music and lights were back at full blast, and the dancers were shaking and stomping as he scooped a chair from the wall and planted himself across it in front of Jack Dealer.

Claire could see the revolutionary clearly in profile. The nose was more aquiline than Che's, the chin heavier, the hair shorter and straighter. In fact, she decided, without the gear there would have been little resemblance. The dark glasses now dangled between lazy fingers over the

47

back of the chair and she could see his eyes—they were narrow, not Chinese, but somehow not European. They could have been Red Indian, or, she realized, Mongolian. She nudged Sami.

'Who is he?' she shouted in his ear.

'Genghiz.'

'Of course.'

'It's not his real name, you understand,' he shouted through his cupped hand into her ear. 'But it is a name the young ones like. With the uniform. They like that too. Such things are important.'

Claire wanted to know more but conversation was impossible. Genghiz and Dealer were now almost nose to nose. They seemed pleased to see each other: they slapped each other's shoulders, Genghiz ruffled Dealer's receding hairline, and Dealer threw a mock punch at the revolutionary's nose—they both roared with laughter. Then Genghiz stood up and, followed by Jack, came down the line to be introduced to the expedition. Again Claire was reminded of royalty. For one brief moment she saw the man full face, caught in the jerky light of the strobe so that he appeared like the Mexican leader of the rebels in a silent movie. In the distorting light she did not like what she saw: behind the fancy dress of beret, beard and scarf the eyes were hard, the face square with deep lines running to a mouth that was thin-lipped and mean looking. The gaze was insolent, cold—mentally, as they say, undressing her; the hand that took hers bony, muscular, hard, deliberately squeezing to hurt. Genghiz laughed and turned back to Dealer. Claire could not hear what he said but guessed it to be obscene. She felt her colour rise, but with rage not shame. Then he was gone, back round the floor, behind the disc jockey and through the door by which he had come.

Claire realized that none of the party had sat down but as Genghiz left so they were leaving too, but by the main entrance. Bewildered she followed. They dropped Sami at the ferry. On the way back she tried to ask Robin and Donna about Genghiz—why they had gone to the Red Pasha Club to meet him, who he really was. Donna knew no more than she. Robin was noncommittal, dismissive.

At the Galata Palas the police were waiting for them—a plain clothes man, tired and rather shabby, and four men with riot sticks and guns in white plastic holsters. They were polite but firm. The whole expedition was to be taken down to the Istanbul Belediye for questioning in connection with the bombing of a police jeep late that afternoon. Two policemen had been killed. A Colonel Nur Arslan had just arrived from Ankara and was waiting for them at the Belediye.

Dealer was obstinate and abusive—insisting on seeing a lawyer, the American Consul, and even mentioning Habeas Corpus.

'Why the hell do they think we've got anything to do with the bombing of some police jeep?'

The plain clothes policeman spoke slowly.

'Mr Dealer, the jeep's mission was to collect the samples of substances found in your van and take them from Ipsala to the Forensic Analysis Laboratories.'

He motioned silently to the uniformed men and two of them hustled Dealer up into the street.

The others followed, quickly and quietly.

PART II : NUR, ALP AND MR MUNDHAM

CHAPTER I

From an office in Ankara, Colonel Nur Arslan ran a small department of the national police whose sole concern was cases involving aliens. To this office, as a matter of routine, the officers in charge of frontier posts, airports, and ports reported any circumstances or incidents which seemed unusual or suspicious. For the most part these reports were filed until the foreigners they concerned had left the country, but occasionally a detail would strike Nur, or a recurring pattern in some individual's movements would appear, or there might be the reappearance of a face or a name that had once been familiar. What and when to report was left to each officer's discretion, and Nur had learnt to take more or less note of these reports according to where they came from.

Ahmet Polatli, the officer in charge of the Ipsala post had been useful in the past, and, as a result of an earlier case, had become something of a friend. In spite of the fact that they had not met since that case, the two men maintained a casual correspondence based round Ahmet's reports. Consequently, when Ahmet received very specific instructions from the Third Section or Political Police regarding the entry of the CHAP expedition he did not hesitate to send a photostat copy to Nur.

This photostat reached Nur's desk in Ankara on the day Claire arrived in Trieste and there were three or four aspects of it that puzzled him and made him feel uneasy.

The letter began by listing the members of the expedition, their passport numbers, and the registration numbers of their vehicles. It went on to request Ahmet to take careful note of the contents of the vans, and finally it asked him to offer every consideration to the expedition which was engaged on a merciful and charitable mission. It was signed by Alp Vural, Deputy Director of the Third Section.

Nur rubbed the palms of his hands in his chronically tired eyes, shook a loosely packed, cheap cigarette—a *Bafra*—from its packet and lit it with a battered Zippo lighter. The letter very obviously suggested trouble. In the first place the secret police—Alp Vural—obviously wanted to be sure that whatever the expedition was carrying would be noted by the customs, but not confiscated. This implied that close examination might reveal that it ought to be confiscated. In the second place the detail that Alp knew about the expedition suggested that it was entering the country with, at the very least, the connivance of the secret police; and in the third place Nur, who was not uninformed, recognized the names of Dealer and Bury and he remembered that the link between them was left-wing revolutionary politics. As he read through Alp Vural's instruction a second time his hand almost tightened on it to crumple it up. Two considerations restrained him: the possibility that there was a conspiracy to smuggle illegal material into the country; and the fact that foreigners were involved and foreigners were his business.

He lifted his phone and issued instructions. Lieutenant Gökalp in Istanbul was to proceed to Alexandropolis where he would follow another well-established routine by identifying and, if possible, photographing the members of the expedition while they were still in Greece. His department had long ago learned that visitors who were planning some sort of illegality were often off guard just before crossing the border.

To Ahmet he spoke personally in spite of the fact that a long distance call from Ankara to Ipsala involved time and trouble. After the polite formalities had been exchanged he went to the point, and asked Ahmet to take samples of the medical supplies when the expedition came through. Finally he arranged for these to be picked up at Ipsala by the police and taken to the Forensic Analysis Laboratories in Istanbul. Nur then forgot about the CHAP expedition until six o'clock four days later when he received news of the attack on the jeep from the Chief of the Istanbul Police. By eight o'clock he was on a *Turk Hava Yollari* flight to Istanbul and by half past nine he was in Lieutenant Gökalp's office in the Belediye waiting to see the members of the CHAP expedition.

Colonel Nur was angry and worried. He sat at the desk leafing through photographs of the jeep. They showed from a variety of angles and distances a vehicle that had been as near completely destroyed as is possible. It seemed that it had first been caught in a cross fire of heavy machine gun bullets; that it had skidded, overturned, and ended on its side in a field of sunflowers. There it had been bombed with at least three grenades, and finally it had been set on fire. Of the two men who had been in it very little that was recognizably human remained, and nothing at all of the samples of Panmycin—it was impossible to say whether these had been taken from the jeep or destroyed in the blaze.

For a time Nur found it difficult to think clearly. The destruction of the jeep seemed wanton, absurd—the work of disturbed children; the loss of life was an obscenity. There had been no need for it—it would have been possible to attack the jeep and take the Panmycin without such

53

savage killing. The added horror was that incidents of this sort had become almost common in the previous six months and Nur shared the opinion of the Istanbul police that this was the work of a particularly vicious group whose leader called himself Genghiz.

Nur tore off the corner of a pack of Bafra cigarettes, shook one out and lit it. If the situation had been simpler there might have been a shred of hope in it: as the Istanbul police had said—the incident appeared to establish a connection between the CHAP expedition and Genghiz's commando, a lead that might be productive. But what the local police did not know, and what Nur could not very well forget, was the connection between the expedition and the Political Police. As this gnawing thought recurred Nur stood up restlessly and paced round the desk; he smoked for a moment and then stubbed out the half-finished butt in the tin ash-tray. Only Allah or the devil would know what the connection meant, but one thing was sure—it meant trouble. It would only be a matter of time before pressure would be brought on Nur, and, he knew from experience, pressure from the Political Police nearly always implied some sort of illegal activity. The only good thing, if it was good, and a shadow of a sardonic smile crossed Nur's mouth, was that the original instruction to Ahmet had come from Alp Vural. Nur had known Alp Vural for a long time. He distrusted him deeply, but he respected him too, and once or twice they had worked well together. But in the meantime he must do what he could before Alp interfered to help the Istanbul Police track down the murderers who had attacked the jeep.

He returned to the desk and looked over a second set of photographs—three in all. He matched them with the five passports that had already been taken from the Galata Palas Hotel.

The first picture showed Robin Bury and Donna Liss at a café table. Both appeared to know that their photograph was being taken. Bury looked angry: he was lifting a card, the menu perhaps, or a folded map, as if to hide his face. Well, that might be significant. The girl had a hand to her hair to push it back and her face was neatly angled—an innocent pose, Nur thought, if vain. The one of Booker Jones and Dealer was poor: both faces were almost completely turned away from the camera as they went into the doctor's doorway. But the Greek doctor himself had been interesting. Lieutenant Gökalp, posing as a sufferer from dyspepsia, had found him old and garrulous. Booker Jones had apparently had a knife wound in his arm and that had been clumsily stitched only a matter of hours before. The doctor had wondered if he should tell the police.

Nur's reactions to the photograph of Claire were very mixed. At first he had been shocked—he had assumed that the girl's swimsuit was deliberately see-through—he had vaguely heard that such garments were worn in the West. But her expression—one of embarrassed anger—was obviously sincere, and Gökalp had described with some shame how he had come to take the picture; her passport photo, too, showed a frank, open face that was definitely pleasing. Nur felt that somehow she was different from the others, that she did not quite fit: she looked so normal, so ordinary; and this he found painful. He did not like to think of her being caught up unaware and innocent in a conspiracy that had already killed two people.

Distantly he heard footsteps and talk from the end of the long corridor. So they were here. Which to interview first? If Claire Mundham really did not know what was going on she would at least tell the truth as far as she knew it, and through her he might be able to trap the men into contradictions.

When Claire found herself facing Colonel Nur her first

feeling was one of relief. She saw a tall man with a kind face that once might have been handsome but was now anxious, and lined with chronic tiredness. She had no idea of his age except that he was 'getting on a bit' but was not as old as her father. He seemed more like a doctor or a school-teacher than a policeman, and, frightened though she had been, she felt almost comforted as he shook hands, introduced himself, and made her sit down.

She refused one of his cigarettes, but liked the way he lit his, the way the black tobacco curled in the bright orange flame, and the smell of the smoke—like Gauloise, but sweeter.

'Now, first tell me about this expedition,' he suggested.

'Well, we're going to Bangladesh, with this new medicine—Panmycin. It's a cure for cholera...'

Nur let her talk, prompting her delicately whenever she showed signs of drying up, and quite quickly certain half-formed impressions he had already received became clearer. First—the expedition was an absurdity. Who would send life-saving drugs overland in the care of people like Bury and Dealer (leaving aside Jones who did appear to be a doctor), when a plane would get there in a tenth or twentieth of the time? Then there was this 'border' incident, and the contradiction over Jones's wound. Nur found that hard to swallow, although Claire had no doubts. Nur was certain that the Panmycin, or whatever, had not come from Bulgaria, but he also felt sure that Claire would go on maintaining it had, even in the face of cross-examination.

And, as he watched her and listened to her prattling on, he felt he was beginning to understand how she fitted in. What the other four were up to he might find out later, but he felt more and more certain that this girl was not up to anything, and that her very innocence was therefore a part of the plot. At some stage, she would be asked to testify, for example, that the Panmycin had come from

Bulgaria—and, because of her obvious innocence, she would be believed.

When she had gone, he lit another Bafra and called for a glass of the milkless tea which is permanently available in all Turkish offices. As the sugar dissolved in the tulip shaped glass he considered who to take next and what his approach would be. Then, just as he was about to send for Bury the phone rang. There was a pause while a connection was made with Ankara and then he heard the deep, gravelly voice of Alp Vural, Deputy Director of the Political Police.

Their conversation was short. Alp first of all established what had happened and why Nur had intervened. He ordered that Nur should conduct no more interviews, but, and this surprised Nur, he said that the members of the expedition should remain in the Belediye cells. Finally he would be in Istanbul himself late the following morning, and he would see Nur then.

Nur felt angry and frustrated, and when, a moment later, the phone rang and he learnt that the press were asking if they could report the detention of the expedition in the following morning's papers, he agreed. His hands had been tied, but he felt it was the least he could do for Claire Mundham.

CHAPTER II

Claire had not needed her father's permission to go on the Bangladesh expedition: she had needed his approval. The evening of the day of her interview with CHAP had been her mother's pottery evening which was fortunate since she wanted her father on her own: not because she expected her mother to make a fuss, but because she wanted her father to herself. Dimly she was aware that this was, in a sense, the story of her life. An older brother, now married, had monopolized her father's attention through most of her childhood, and she still felt a need to push herself into her father's consciousness, to demand attention, almost to dare him to refuse approval.

He was a big man with broad shoulders and a barrel chest which gave solidity to his voice. Now nearly sixty— he had come to Mrs Mundham late after an earlier, childless marriage—he was beginning to show signs of age beyond his years. His hearing was not always perfect, his cheeks were jowly, his greying hair not too kempt and definitely receding. He slept often at weekends and in front of the television, or even in their old Cortina (he could have afforded a much newer and larger car, but was not interested) when he took them down to the Thames estuary with their powered inflatable on the roof rack. This craft had been one of his few toys, but recently his interest had begun to wane. He had taken over the management of the small publishing firm he had worked with for years and instead of retirement he was now faced with at least five more years' hard work. The firm published technical handbooks for do-it-yourself enthusiasts. He had been just too old to be a combat pilot during the war, but since he had learnt to fly in the twenties, he had been an instructor, and later reached Group Captain.

Now, as the theme of 'The Virginian' came up Claire had turned off the television and sat down opposite him.

'I want to talk to you.'

'And I want the news.'

'Before Mum comes home.'

'Just as you say, dear.' He sipped his scotch.

'I've joined an expedition to Bangladesh, with medical supplies.'

'They'll be very grateful.'

'Yes, I know. But do you mind?'

'Tell me about it.'

She had told, but tried to play down her growing enthusiasm for Robin Bury. The result was that Mr Mundham at first thought that she had fallen for the clergyman, and then that he was in danger of ending up with Jack Dealer as a son-in-law.

'This Dealer chap?' he had asked.

'Oh, I didn't really like him. He seemed hard.'

This was said with obvious sincerity, and he finished his whisky.

Mr Mundham had heard her out and at the end could think of nothing to say but, 'Just as you say, dear,' which was all that Claire really expected, though she wanted more. In fact Mr Mundham had a lot more to say, but was conscious of being about ten years too late. He was extremely fond of his daughter, always had been, but he was an undemonstrative man who could find no way of expressing the depth of his concern for those he loved beyond allowing them to do exactly what they wanted, fitting in with their wishes, and picking up the pieces when their plans went wrong. He had gone to bed an anxious man, but neither his wife nor his daughter would have guessed.

In the few days between this conversation and Claire's departure little had happened to reassure him. He too had wondered why supplies for Bangladesh could not more usefully be flown out, and because this thought disturbed him he had made enquiries about Bury and Dealer. He had discovered that Bury had indeed resigned from his lectureship but that it had been only a matter of time before his resignation would have been asked for: complaints had been received that he had been using his position as a political platform and that he had been openly advocating politics of violence. Mr Mundham was a completely unpolitical person—sincerely so rather than out of laziness: he would have happily conceded to anyone the right to hold any views however extreme. What he did not like was that his daughter might be mixed up with people quite close to groups like the 'Angry Brigade', perhaps close enough, so he gathered from his acquaintances, to be held as an accessory.

Nor had he liked what he had heard about Dealer—an old friend of his who was the representative in England of a large American publishing firm had quite a lot to say on the subject. Dealer had enjoyed a few years of fame and prosperity in the late fifties and early sixties, until Beatlemania had thrust him and other Rock soloists out of the limelight. There had followed a few years of obscurity, but in the late sixties he had reappeared in the Civil Rights movement, in Paris in '68, and in the Anti-War movement, singing and marching. A book had appeared under his name called *My Right to Rock*. None of this was all that bad—Dealer did not have a drink problem, did not take drugs, nor was he a womanizer. However, Mr Mundham's friend had heard a rumour that the hard core of the protest movement had rejected him and that long ago, when he had still been a longshoreman in San Diego, he had served a short prison sentence for assaulting and nearly killing a picket during a strike. In short, before he achieved fame as a singer it seemed possible that he had been employed as a strikebreaker.

Again, although he disliked violence, Mr Mundham would have felt it to be presumptuous to make a judgement about a man without hearing his side of the story, but what left him uneasy was the apparent contradictions in the man, and also a sense that, in spite of at least seeming to share radical politics, Bury and Dealer were ill-assorted.

He had taken Claire to Victoria to see her off and then, as the last carriage of the train disappeared, his unease had come to a head and he decided to call on CHAP.

The Reverend Frere answered the door himself. He was in shirt sleeves and his dog-collar had come adrift over his black dicky. He led the way up the stairs, past the painting of 'Hope' and into the front room where Claire had been interviewed. It was now impossibly untidy with books, papers, magazines—one or two of which were rather worldly for a clergyman—strewn about the place. Although it was half past eleven Frere appeared to be in the middle of his breakfast: there were an egg-cup, egg-shells, toast on the desk, and a large cracked coffee cup still steamed. These were cleared away into a backroom which seemed to be a sort of kitchen, to half-intoned cries of 'Do sit down, what a mess you've caught me in. Oh no please don't apologize, my fault entirely, even the bed's not made.' The last referred to the sofa that Claire had struggled with, and which was now serving as a divan. At last Frere was safely behind the desk and ready to give his attention to his visitor.

'Now, Mr ... I'n afraid I've quite forgotten what you said your name was, such a failing and a handicap in one of my calling, what can I do for you?'

'Mundham. Mundham. Er, I understand these are the offices of CHAP.'

'CHAP? CHAP? Yes, of course. Christian Help for Asiatic Peoples, to be sure. I do sometimes forget though they do help me handsomely: in fact they pay the rent on these rooms—entirely, the rates and all.'

'Er, sometimes forget?' Mr Mundham's unease grew and he walked slowly round to the window.

'Well you know, I only hear from them perhaps twice a year at the most and then it is quite a nuisance because I do have to follow quite detailed.... My goodness gracious me, how silly of me, Mr Mundham, I remember now, and it can't have been much more than a week ago. You must be ...?'

He left the question hopefully in the air and Mr Mundham turned to face him as he supplied the answer.

'Claire's father.'

'Of course, yes indeed. Such a charming girl, such poise and natural good manners, so rare nowadays, and so dedicated to helping our poor friends in Vietnam.'

'Bangladesh.'

'Bless you.'

'No—I said Bangladesh, not Vietnam.'

'Really? Yes, of course, how silly of me. It was North Vietnam the time before that they called on me.'

'Who called on you?'

'CHAP.'

'Ah yes, I see.'

But he didn't see. The interview had continued in the same breathless confused way for a further twenty minutes before Mr Mundham finally gave up seeking the reassurance he had hoped to find. Indeed one or two aspects served to leave him even more disturbed than he had been.

For instance it appeared that the Reverend Frere had not even placed the advertisement in the *New Statesman*, that he had sent all the replies to it to another address, that he had been told to receive Dealer and Bury on the day of the interview, that Claire had been the only girl interviewed.

Mr Mundham picked up his hat and, rather wearily, asked his last question.

'Mr Frere, could you tell me the address you write to or forward CHAP mail to.'

'Ah ... no.' The clergyman's eyes sought help in the ceiling, and then in the waste paper basket to Mr Mundham's left, and finally from his own toes. He clasped and unclasped his hands. 'Ah ... no. That would be quite improper.'

'Improper?'

'Well, they have, you see, enjoined me quite strictly not to divulge their address. No doubt the good people do not wish their charities to be divulged. In almsgiving one does not want one's left hand to know what one's right is doing, is not that what Our Good Lord told us?'

A week later the *Guardian* carried a brief agencied report that Jack Dealer, the protest singer, and Robin Bury, together with friends with whom they were travelling, were being held for questioning in Istanbul. The police had given no reasons but it was widely assumed that their detention was in connection with Left Wing activities. Following the recent bombings in the city many prominent Turks, particularly academics, with known Left Wing sympathies, had been arrested. However, this was the first time that foreigners had been detained in this context.

Mr Mundham had maintained many of the friendships he had made during his war service in the R.A.F. He was also, when occasion demanded it, a determined man who could act with an almost ruthless efficiency. A very senior executive at B.E.A. had served with him and at eleven o'clock on the same day he was on a scheduled flight to Istanbul. The plane had been held for forty minutes for him. In Istanbul his methods were equally forthright. He went straight to the Consulate and there he was told that his daughter was still in police custody, and there was absolutely no chance of seeing her or indeed of seeing the police officers in charge of the enquiry. The Consul had already done all that he could—he could assure Mr Mundham that Claire was in good health, and that there was little likelihood of her being charged. Under Turkish law she could be held on a warrant issued by an examining magistrate for several days without being charged while enquiries were being made and, until she was charged or, which was more likely, released, there was little hope that Mr Mundham would be allowed to see her.

The B.E.A. executive had also told him that the son of a mutual friend was air attaché at the British Embassy in Ankara. Mr Mundham remembered that he himself had attended the family party when this son had passed out of Cranford. He booked into the Park Hotel (again on his friend's recommendation) and patiently pursued the air attaché by telephone to his home in Ankara. Naturally, the air attaché was most sympathetic, would do what he could. Two hours later, it was seven o'clock in the evening, he rang back. The man Mr Mundham should try to see was Colonel Nur Arslan. From all accounts a very decent sort of chap, a policeman who always looked into cases involving foreigners. Usually he was to be found at the Ministry of the Interior in Ankara, but, it appeared, he was at that moment at the Belediye in Istanbul.

Mr Mundham took a taxi to the Belediye.

CHAPTER III

Deputy Director Alp Vural was very angry at Colonel Nur's intervention in the affairs of the Bangladesh expedition. Travelling overnight on the Wagons-Lit Express from Ankara had not improved his temper but at least it had not terrified him as flying would have done. He arrived in Colonel Nur's office shortly before lunch on the day following the bombing of the jeep and immediately tried to take over, but Colonel Nur was not going to be so easily moved. He remained firmly on his side of the desk and looked across it at his old acquaintance, colleague and adversary.

Alp Vural was a large ruin of a man. Ten years older than Nur, he was several pounds overweight; his face was grey and had collapsed into pouches and purses of flabby flesh; his hair was a dirty sort of white and very thin. Yet his eyes retained a light of real intelligence, frequently touched with a cheeky humour. Alp Vural was a fixer—to survive in his job he needed to be. He smoked all the time, drank *raki* or whisky whenever he could, and spoke with the deep, gravelly voice of the chronic bronchitic, pausing often to gasp in mouthfuls of air. He carried rank far senior to Nur's.

'I should order you back to Ankara,' he rasped after perfunctorily shaking hands. 'Your interference is a confounded nuisance.'

'But you won't.' A slight smile lit Nur's eyes.

'Why are you so sure that I will let you stay? Stop ...

65

Before you answer, send for some iced water.'

Alp lowered himself into a cane armchair that creaked beneath him, and produced a half bottle of raki from his brief case. He poured a measure into a glass of the water when it had come and watched it turn cloudy.

'Now...?'

'You will not risk offending me while there is a possibility that I may be of use to you. These people are foreigners. My department not only has responsibility for them, a responsibility you would have to persuade the Minister to revoke...'

'That could be arranged.'

'... it also has the expertise to deal with them. We can supply you with interpreters, handle the Consulates for you, and the foreign press.'

'All right, good,' Alp chuckled and coughed, 'we still understand each other and we should be able to work together again.'

'I am not sure about that,' Nur lit a Bafra. 'I shall want to know first just what is going on.'

'Nur bey, you cannot possibly think I am going to tell you very much.' Alp swirled ice and raki round his tumbler before draining it. 'I don't know it all myself. I think it would be best if you told me what you know, why you interfered, and I will then tell you as much of the rest as you need to know.'

Nur smoked for a moment. 'Right,' he said, at last. 'This expedition is not what it seems. I know your department is involved, I think it is part of a plan directed against the Left wing movement, and particularly the commando led by Genghiz. Because foreigners are involved I tried to find out more about it; because I suspected that there was something illegal about the Panmycin I suggested that the Customs at Ipsala should take samples. Because of that the jeep was attacked and two men were killed. You could have warned me, you know, indeed you should

66

have done ... Let that go for the moment. Let me go on, I am only thinking aloud. The samples were taken. They were destroyed in the jeep ... How did the terrorists know they were in that jeep?'

Alp remained motionless. Nur arrived at the answer to his question.

'Because the information was leaked to them. You are not usually so callous.'

'It would not have done to have them attacking every police vehicle between Istanbul and the frontier.'

Nur's hand shook as he lit another Bafra.

'Nevertheless,' he went on, 'you deliberately let those men die. You cannot expect me to like it: it is against law, decency, all the things we are meant to maintain and protect ...'

For a moment Alp looked angry again; then he poured more raki on the tired ice cubes at the bottom of his glass.

'Nur bey, don't preach at me. Last March the elected government was dismissed by the Army because of its failure to deal with Left wing terrorism. Since then journalists, artists, professors have been arrested and held without trial, but at least we still have a civilian government, and we may yet return to democracy. But only if the present government destroys the Left Wing movement. If it fails the argument for a military dictatorship, for mass internment, for concentration camps, for suppression of the press, for torture, becomes unanswerable.' He drank again and his voice softened. 'Nur bey, we are friends, we believe in the same things. I am acting in the national interest and with the highest authority behind me. Now, you must do as I say, and not act without reference to me again. You can do nothing to protect these foreigners— you could put them in further danger.'

'What they are doing is dangerous, then?'

'Of course.' Alp raised a hand to forestall interruption.

'But you must not worry about them. To a greater or lesser extent they know what they are doing. They must be ready for some trouble, some risk, even if it does not come from the quarter they expect.'

'And this is true of all of them? You are telling me that none of them believes they are going to Bangladesh?'

Alp hesitated and his shoulder lifted in the slightest of twitches as he gazed into his half empty glass.

'I think perhaps there is still one who expects to go to India. But only one. Of the other four, well, who knows? They are either romantics who think they are furthering the cause of universal brotherhood by mixing with psychopaths like Genghiz, or they know most of what it is all about, they are professionals like us, and can take care of themselves.'

Nur's hand came down on the desk. 'And the one? He or she is expendable, like those two policemen?'

Alp shrugged. 'In every struggle people will get hurt. But remember, if we win, there will be few; if we lose, many. In the meantime they are safe enough in the cells here, and it is good that they are here. Genghiz would have been suspicious if we had taken no action at all against them after the bombing of the jeep. Now you must excuse me. I have much to see to, and people to talk to to see what to do about this new situation. I'll be in touch with you late tomorrow.'

He hauled himself to his feet and the smoke swirled around him.

'I'll see myself out.'

For the next thirty hours or so Nur busied himself with routine matters, but the problem of the expedition and particularly of Claire Mundham was always in the front of his mind. He had himself deduced Claire's innocence and Alp had more or less corroborated it. As the next day wore on he arrived at a resolution to make Claire's release and her return to England the price of his co-operation with Alp. All afternoon he waited to hear from the Deputy Director but no message came. Then, just as he was thinking of leaving the Belediye for the evening and returning to the nearby hotel which he used on his rare trips to Istanbul, he received a call from the duty desk. An Englishman, Mr Mundham, was waiting below and wanted to see him. Nur asked for him to be shown up.

Nur saw, as he held out his hand, a well-built man with iron-grey hair receding behind a high forehead, a grey face heavily lined, a square jaw. He received an impression of strength that was softened by warm eyes, and a mouth not weak, but far from severe. The hand that grasped his was large and strong but not assertive. Nur offered him a cigarette. Mr Mundham was plainly ill at ease and Nur judged him to be a shy man—and very tired too.

'You must be Claire Mundham's father?'

'Er, yes. She's my, um, only daughter. I'm sorry if she's been a nuisance to you.' Mr Mundham smiled faintly.

Nur thought the 'er's' and 'um's' of Mr Mundham's speech were due to nervousness—only when he knew him better did he realize that they were habitual mannerisms; as also was his habit of deprecating his family with affectionate grimness.

'You got here very soon. You must have started as soon as the English press got hold of the story, and in less than twenty-four hours you have found me. That is good going.'

Mr Mundham deprecatingly described how he had been helped by old friends.

Nur looked at his papers and stubbed out his cigarette. There was a pause, then both spoke at once.

'Would you like some tea?'

'Look, if I'm being a nuisance...'

69

'Sorry.'

'No, not at all, after you.'

'Would you like some tea?'

'Er, yes, that is, if it's no trouble.'

'None at all.' Nur rang a hand-bell, and presently an old man with close-cropped hair and wearing blue overalls appeared with two small tulip-shaped glasses of milkless tea on a copper tray.

Mr Mundham sipped.

'Very, um, refreshing. Not unlike Russian tea.'

'I'm afraid I'm almost an addict. We'll have some more soon. Now. You must be very worried about Claire.'

'Yes, yes. And, um, my wife is too, of course.'

'Of course.'

'But I don't want you to misunderstand me. If she has done anything wrong we must, um, see it through. And of course I don't want to take up your time. The air attaché said you were the head man for cases of this sort and you must be very busy. If you'd like to pass me on to an underling I shan't mind at all. But the main thing is...' a note of determination, of the will that lay beneath the gentle manner, intruded, '... I should like to see my daughter. I expect she would like someone to hold her hand, to know there is someone familiar around while the law takes its course.'

Since Nur believed that it was unlikely, as things stood, that the law would take its course, this remark was more disturbing than Mr Mundham guessed.

'Mr Mundham, tell me about your daughter.'

Mr Mundham cleared his throat, which had not reacted well to the unfamiliar tobacco.

'Claire is a nice girl. But scatterbrained, naïve, impulsive. Yet, from her school record quite clever and talented. I think she is rather easily led: she had a spot of trouble in Spain just over a year ago. Not her fault at all, but she rather misjudged the, er, reliability of the man she was with. I'm afraid she had rather a spoiled and protected childhood.'

'Politics? I should say the background to this business is political.'

'None as far as I know. Except a vague desire to help underdogs. That is why she is going to Bangladesh.'

'There are indications that the organizers of the Expedition do not intend it to get anywhere near Bangladesh.'

Mr Mundham looked up with surprise and then anxiety. 'I'm quite sure that is where Claire thought she was going.'

'Yes, I think you're right.' Nur picked up a ball-point and stabbed at the blotter on the desk. 'Mr Mundham, I will try to do what is right for your daughter, but there are difficulties that you are not aware of. I am sorry I cannot let you see her tonight, or at least not until I have seen a senior officer who is concerned with the case.' He stood up and took Mr Mundham to the door. 'Please rest assured. As far as I know your daughter has done nothing wrong, and I am going to do everything I can to have her released as soon as possible. In the meantime I can get in touch with you at your hotel. The Park? Good.'

After Mr Mundham had gone he sat down to smoke one more cigarette and found that his determination to get Claire out of the expedition and safely home with her father had hardened considerably.

The phone rang.

CHAPTER IV

'Nur bey?' The gravelly voice held a note of urgency. 'I am glad you are still there. I am in the office of my Third Section colleague here in the Belediye. Could you come down immediately?'

Nur took a lift, walked along a wider corridor than his own and into a far more spacious office. Alp was behind the desk with wreaths of cigar smoke around him and a bottle of Teacher's in front of him. Only about an eighth had been drunk.

'Good, you came quickly,' Alp grunted. 'Have a whisky —a present from my very good American friend and colleague Mr Arnold Bitterne.'

Nur half turned and found himself face to face with a tall man, bespectacled, nearly bald but what hair there was was gingery, and dressed in a pale grey jacket over check trousers. Nur realized as he shook hands that the American had remained behind the still open door almost as if he was hiding.

Although Nur rarely drank he accepted the Teacher's. He and Bitterne sat facing each other at each end of the desk, and almost before he could get the glass to his lips, the American was talking.

'Colonel Arslan,' Bitterne spoke with a high voice, and his heavily freckled hands flapped nervously and often, 'I guess you must be wondering who I am, and why I'm here, and I guess it's only right I should apologize that I haven't been in touch with you before. Deputy Director

Vural tells me you feel you should have been in the picture earlier.'

'If I had been, two dead policemen would still be alive.'

'Yes, I guess that's so. And you are quite right to press that point home, and it certainly was a miscalculation on our part not to inform you. Well, that's what I propose to do right now. Director Gunay of the Third Section concurred with me that although it is not normal practice for control to be known to his operatives, we could waive a point in view of the circumstances, particularly since we may need your willing co-operation in the next few weeks.'

Nur made very little of all this.

'Certainly I shall be able to co-operate more usefully when I do know what it is all about,' he said drily.

'That is very self-evident.' Bitterne punctuated this with a nervous high laugh. 'Well, what we have in mind is very simple. The cases in Dealer's van contain substances that the guerrillas would find very, very useful. We are trying to tempt them out to accept them in such a way that your forces of law and, er, order can catch them. The problem has been, and remains, to persuade your guerrillas that the offer of these materials is a genuine one. To overcome this problem we have elaborated the original considerably.' Bitterne paused. 'Are you with me?'

'Like making it appear that the cases came from Bulgaria.'

'I see you can follow the logic of the operation. Now, further to that end, we have a plan to supply Panmycin to your dissident Kurds in the East . . .'

Alp shifted uneasily and noisily drank some whisky.

'. . . the Deputy Director does not think this is necessary,' the hand flapped and Bitterne hurried on, 'but we feel sure that the guerrillas will accept the bonafides of people who have helped the Kurds in this way . . .'

Alp emitted an explosive cough.

'Arnold bey,' he rasped, 'it really will not do. Urban

guerrillas in Istanbul have no interest in nomadic shepherds eight hundred miles away.' He leant forward and spoke earnestly. 'Look. Your original plan could really do a lot of harm to the Left Wing movement. It may even help to keep the civilian government in power. Now there are plenty of officers who look forward to a time when a military coup would be possible. So, if they get wind of this operation, they will try to stop it. The East is practically a military zone: it is not possible for three orange vans to move about, meeting Kurds, without the army seeing them. Look. We've got the stuff here in Istanbul. Genghiz is nibbling. Let's get on with it.'

Bitterne's head shifted from side to side and his eyes rolled redly behind his spectacles.

'No, Alp bey,' he said, and Nur caught a note of desperation in his voice, 'Director Gunay and I have been all over this ground many times, and it is quite decided that the expedition goes East and hands over some Panmycin to the Kurds. I really do see this as quite an important part of the operation.' He calmed down. 'Now, Colonel Nur, you have, in outline, what the CHAP expedition is about. Can we count on your help if we need it?'

Nur considered. In fact he knew very little: there were many unanswered questions in his mind, but he felt he had been told all and perhaps rather more than Bitterne wanted him to know. In the meantime co-operating would do no harm, and it would keep him in touch.

'I'm not sure I see how I can help you,' he said, 'but if you think I can I will. But I should like to raise the position of Claire Mundham in all this.'

'I don't follow you.' Bitterne's voice struck a harder note.

'I am sure Claire Mundham thinks she is going to Bangladesh. She is, in other words, involved in something very dangerous, unknowingly. Her father has just arrived in Istanbul ...'

74

'You let the press know,' Alp rumbled. 'You had no business to do that.'

'... he is very anxious about her and is ready to take her home. I think she should go back to England.'

'That is quite impossible.' The glasses flashed round the room again. 'Genghiz has seen her. To break up the expedition now might easily frighten him off. Probably her innocence is one of the reasons why he is showing interest in the expedition. No. She must stay on.'

'Mr Mundham will not like that. And his hands are not tied. He can go to the press, or he could simply find the expedition when you release them, walk up to Claire and take her home.'

There was a long moment of silence. Neither Alp nor Bitterne would look at Nur, and he felt cold fingers touch his spine. At last Bitterne raised his head and looked at Alp who nodded briefly. Bitterne turned back to Nur. His voice was cold.

'Mr Mundham's arrival in this country is a great embarrassment. And it is because I felt you could help us to avoid any drastic action against him that I have come here to see you. We cannot arrest Mr Mundham. Equally, we cannot now allow him to remain free. Nor can we let him return to England where he would have access to his Foreign Office and the British Press. So. We must ask you to look after him. Perhaps you will tell him just a little of what we have told you, but in a reassuring way. Take him back to Ankara with you if you like, but, whatever else you do, convince him that any unconsidered action will put his life and his daughter's in real danger. Do you understand?'

Nur looked at the American with incredulity.

'I understand,' he said at last, and there was loathing in his voice. 'At least I suppose I do.' He looked at Alp. 'Is that really how it is?'

Alp nodded. 'That's how it is,' he rasped.

PART III : CLAIRE AGAIN

CHAPTER I

'Why have we taken the road east instead of south?' asked Claire, as they drove out of Diyarbekir four days later.

Robin felt a coldness in the pit of his stomach and he gripped the steering wheel a little tighter. This is it, he thought. He noted that her voice held no alarm, only curiosity, and he reckoned he might be able to hold her off a little longer: the nearer the rendezvous they were when she learnt the truth the better.

'We're taking the frontier right on the corner, where Iraq, Iran, and Turkey meet. A place called Semdinli. The roads are worse but it saves between two and three hundred miles.'

In the corner of his eye he could see her reaching for guide books and a more detailed map than the one she had been following. He risked a glance at her and felt a pang of emotion as he did. Claire really had been rather marvellous. When the police returned them to the Galata Palas she had been calm, though obviously relieved as well; Donna on the other hand had been near hysterical demanding that she and Booker should return to Chatham N.Y. But by the morning Booker had calmed her and they were able to set off for Ankara.

The party had remained in a bad mood. They had been followed, stopped twice at roadblocks—once by the police and once by the army; they were all tired, nervous and edgy. From Ankara on the country was comfortless: huge spaces, near desert, hot windswept steppe alleviated only occasionally by drab, dusty villages of dunghuts, and, once, by a nightmarish landscape carved out of volcanic tufa— fairy chimneys with boulders balanced on pinnacles and hovels carved out of the soft cliff faces. Yet Claire's mood had improved. She seemed to like the emptiness, the barrenness, and the dry, hot, dusty winds, though she had to double her dosage of Booker's pills when the fine tufa dust penetrated the air cooling vents.

Jack Dealer, too, had brightened as they headed east across the Anatolian plateau. They had stopped at a well the day before and he had begun to fool about, shouting and running across the plain after dust devils, and halloo-ing at the blood red sun like an overweight werewolf. But his change of mood Robin put down not to love of deserts but to the fact that they were no longer being followed and that they were within half a day of the rendezvous, the moment when they would cease to be the CHAP expedition to Bangladesh.

How would Claire take it?

She really was delightful. Day after day she had sat next to him, the maps spread over the thin cotton of the smock she wore, the bridge of her nose reddening and then peeling, freckles sharpening up on cheekbones and on the backs of her small delicate hands. What a fascinat-ing mixture she was: sometimes girlish, rattling on about school or her father; then besting him in more or less intellectual argument; and two nights ago sketching him rapidly as they waited for their meal in a cheap hotel. It had been a good likeness, and disturbing, perceptive. She had managed to suggest the loneliness behind the aca-demic seriousness of his eyes.

Only once or twice had she made references to her nine months of hippy-style wandering and he had felt some-thing melt in him at the half-concealed suggestion that she had been hurt. And he could not help wondering what she had been like as a man's lover—even the arrogant

78

lout's that she had managed to get entangled with. This will not do, thought Robin, and he pummelled the horn at a villager on a donkey.

The road was climbing away from the plain of Diyarbekir back into the mountains of the Eastern Taurus. Vast crags, snowcapped against the pale limpid sky of early morning flashed in the distance between nearer tree-clad peaks. It was a bleak but imposing landscape, larger than life: every boulder, every fissured cliff seemed too big, dwarfing the scraps of pasture and the stone-built villages clustered round their minarets. Robin looked at the milometer. Five more miles, say seven or eight minutes, then the fork to the north and the showdown.

'We can't cross at Semdinli.'

'Whyever not?'

'It's in a military zone. We need special permits from the military. It says so here. In the guide.'

'I ... I expect Jack's got them. Or knows he can get them. The papers I mean.'

She was silent for a minute, but Robin could sense her uneasiness.

'I bet he hasn't got any papers. And after Istanbul, he won't get them.'

He grunted noncommittally, his eyes already searching for the turn to the left ahead.

'This is stupid. I think we should turn back. Back to Diyarbekir and the road to Mardin. The post at Nusayhin is the proper one. It says so quite clearly.'

There it was. He pulled in and set the indicator winking, slowed down.

'You are stopping then. I'm sure it would be better. Ask the others...'

But he swung the Volkswagen off the main road, accelerated, and changed back into top. The tyres drummed over the unmetalled surface and they began to sway as the suspension absorbed the appalling mixture

79

of boulders, grit and ruts. Claire glanced behind: the headlights of Dealer's van glowed through the dense clouds that were now spewing out behind them.

'What on earth are you doing?'

'Hold on, old girl.'

'Old girl! What is this? Robin for God's sake, where are we going?'

'Look old ... I mean, hang on. I'll explain, but not just yet. This bloody track needs all my attention.'

Indeed, it had almost disappeared, picking its way round outcrops of rock, dusty scrub, and drumming over the smooth pebbles of a dried out water course.

'Then bloody well slow down.'

Robin did, although he did not want to. It had been in his mind to get as far from the main road, as near to the rendezvous as he could before beginning any sort of explanation.

'Now stop, and tell me what is going on.'

Robin drove on—his teeth remained gritted.

'Well, for heaven's sake say something. But keep your eye on the track.'

'Claire,' he said at last—he had to speak loudly, almost shout above the racket of flying scree, 'Claire, in about ten miles we're going to meet a clan of Kurds. Do you know about Kurds?'

'Nomads—black tents, never settled down to village life —yes, I know about them. But that's fine, I'd love to meet some Kurds. Why the secrecy and drama?'

'We're not going to Bangladesh. The Panmycin is for the Kurds, to help them to keep the right to be nomads, not only here but in Iraq, Iran, and even Russia.'

Claire was stunned: questions formed and dissolved in her mind; the track went on unfolding to a cacophony like stones rattled in a biscuit tin; the van seemed very small, she felt shut in, trapped. Robin seemed a stranger. Tears pricked at her eyes and as she was holding on to the safety handles she could do nothing about it. Her nose began to run.

'I expect you're wondering why I'm telling you now, why I didn't tell you before, right at the beginning.'

She sniffed. At some risk he managed to pull a handful of Kleenex from the dashboard shelf and thrust them into her lap.

'It's dangerous, that's why. If we're caught we'll be in very serious trouble. We'll be lucky to get away with being deported. To the Turks the Kurds are a threat, possible guerrillas. Already the Left, the Turkish Liberation Army, has made contact with them. And so we thought it best you should not know until the last possible moment.'

'"We"? Then the others know?' Her sense of being lost increased.

'Donna perhaps doesn't. We left it to Booker to decide when to tell her.'

'But why take Donna and me with you?'

'Dealer thought that the three of us were too well known internationally as radicals, for the Turks to let us in on our own. But with two ordinary girls, with no reputation or record, we thought we might stand a chance. Especially we thought we might be questioned and with two girls amongst us, quite convinced we were on our way to Bangladesh, with no chance of you being inconsistent in your answers, or anything like that.... One thing: if we are caught, we shall insist that you and Donna are innocent and knew nothing about our real intentions.'

Claire heaved a deep sigh which ended in a shudder.

'All right then. But why the Kurds? Why is their need greater than the children's in Bangladesh?'

'The world knows about Bangladesh, and cares. Not only all the big charities, but governments too. Aid may move slowly, but our three cases of Panmycin would be a drop in the ocean that is already getting out to Dacca.

But few people know about the Kurds, and no-one cares. They need Panmycin too. News reached us in London that both the Turks and the Arabs were poisoning their wells. Jack Dealer wanted to take arms but Brer Frere at CHAP drew the line at that, and I would have done too. We're simply helping them to resist the oldest and cruellest form of biological warfare known to man.'

This was persuasive—especially the bit about poisoned wells—though, in spite of her confusion and everything else, Claire dimly perceived a note of over-blown rhetoric at the end. She sniffed again, and Robin went on quickly.

'I'm sorry if I'm addressing you like a political meeting. I suppose it's just a habit—I've done it too often. And it is difficult explaining and trying to keep this thing in one piece at the same time.'

There were more trees now, and more pasture. The track was climbing a wide ravine and Claire thought there must be water near.

'There can't be nine thousand sick Kurds up here,' she said.

'No of course not. We're handing the Panmycin over to the chief of this clan, Booker will show them how to use it, and then it will be distributed right across the steppes and the mountains from here to Samarkand.'

'And what about us?'

'We make our way home, to England.'

'But won't the Turks want to know where we've been and why we haven't gone on?'

'Well we will go on. That is we'll leave Turkey on the Eastern frontier—once out of Turkey we can turn South through Syria and Lebanon into Israel and take a boat back to Greece or Italy.'

Claire still felt unsatisfied, but she could think of no line of questions that would lead anywhere. She was hurt, and disappointed: she wanted to see India, Bengal, the East. The promised trip to the zoo had turned out to be

Saturday afternoon at the local pets' corner.

They swung round a corner and she screamed. In front of them the crags closed in suddenly on the track, making a narrow defile. A tree had been felled across their path, and behind it were horsemen, robed in black, carrying guns. As Robin slammed on the brakes a pony galloped alongside, reared up in front of them, and the bearded warrior on it loosed off a heavy revolver into the air above their heads. The valley was filled with shouts, halloos, and more shots reverberated round the rocks.

CHAPTER II

That evening Claire sat on a boulder at the edge of the camp and felt better. Below her were twelve or thirteen large black tents, woven, she had learnt, from goat hair. Redolent smoke drifted from fires into the clear sharp mountain air, mixing with the odours of pines, cooking, and goats. Further away from her the flocks were grazing on a wide water meadow; she could hear the dull chiming of their bells, and a gentle murmur from the tents, pierced by an occasional laugh or the cry of a child. A small river meandered through the meadow; beyond it trees marched up to scree, and then the mountains—enormous cliffs which darkened from pale grey to blackness except where the invisible sun still shed a rosy glow on the highest peaks and warmed the icy purity of the perpetual snows.

Robin had told her that up there was the small glacier that fed the river, even at the end of the long dry summer. The whole scene was about perfect and she could not help thinking that the nomads fitted into it, were part of it, not alien intruders. As if to point this thought a reedy pipe began to play on the far side of the encampment: a haunting melody, rising and falling and marked by the brittle snap of cane stick on goatskin drum. Only the vans jarred, bringing a touch of 'Le Camping' into the scene. Like all tourists who seek out the strange, the unusual, or the unspoilt, Claire was facing the dilemma that her very presence, which was giving her so much pleasure, was an intrusion and possibly a hostile one. But then she wasn't a tourist, she remembered, and certainly the Panmycin had been welcomed and there seemed to be some need of it.

Their welcome in the defile had not been hostile, merely exuberant. Once Robin and Jack Dealer had identified themselves a calm had fallen and the Expedition had been welcomed with a strange, serious formality, by each of them. Communication had been difficult and remained a problem, although they discovered that the son of the chief had attended High School in Damascus and spoke French well; but for the rest, the Kurds' Iranian dialect remained quite unintelligible—though odd words from both Turkish and Persian phrasebooks got through.

A journey of three hours followed at a pony's pace. They left the track and soon entered this second valley—broad and almost park-like in its lush pastures, light woodland, and pine forests. Claire had had plenty of opportunity to study the six Kurds with them. They were tall thin men, weather-beaten but not dark skinned, heavily moustached with deep set eyes and bushy eyebrows. Their clothes were an odd mixture: four of them wore black, robe-like garments, faintly Arabic in appearance but shorter and less voluminous, over huge baggy trousers which ended just below the knee. Three wore leather gaiters, and the others woollen stockings and army boots. From under the robes heavily embroidered waistcoats glinted with tarnished silver. All were armed—with silver mounted knives, heavy revolvers, rifles thirty or forty years old. Their horses were shaggy, ill-kempt by Claire's suburban standards, but well-fed and hardy. The men looked fierce when they were at all preoccupied, but often they relaxed into shouts of laughter or broad grins which revealed strong teeth.

At last they had come to the yayla or summer pasture. The rest of the clan turned out to meet them—perhaps eighty all told, counting women and children. In the midst, in front of the largest tent, stood a very old man, supported by two equally old women—the Sheikh Ibrahim himself, and to him the members of the expedition were presented by his son, Barzani. They were served with thick coffee in tiny cups with heavy silver cup holders. The coffee was drunk with the heavy formality of the first introductions; then, Sheikh Ibrahim, who said little and was obviously on the edge of senility, bowed and was led into the great tent, leaving them with Barzani. The formal welcome over, the atmosphere changed. The whole clan had gathered round them, the children gazing with wonder, the youths exclaiming over the Volkswagens, the men, led by Barzani, opening and examining the cases of Panmycin with restrained wonder, questioning Booker with eager seriousness about the mysterious vials of white crystals.

Two women—tall, straight, unveiled like all Kurdish women, with chains of gold coins like little suns gleaming across their foreheads—led Claire and Donna around the camp, and at last into one of the tents. Inside Claire was surprised at the number of partitions, cubicles, rooms there seemed to be. The atmosphere was black, heavy with the smell of goat hair, but the furnishings were rich: tiny silver lamps swung above tasselled cushions, rugs and chests. Copper and silver utensils hung from the posts; there were richly inlaid stringed instruments, guns, embroidered robes, and everywhere the dull gleam of oxidized silver in fine filigree. It was like a strangely authentic Aladdin's cave. Claire and Donna were seated on cushions and offered mint tea, hard, dry biscuits, and soft Turkish Delight stuffed with hazel nuts.

As they sipped and chewed in a rather embarrassed silence Claire became aware of an intermittent moaning and whispering from somewhere at the back of the tent. She must have glanced towards it for after a time one of the Kurdish women rose and touched her on the shoulder, beckoning to her and Donna. They pushed through woven hangings into the furthest recesses in the tent, to the darkest enclosure of all, a tiny cell lit by only two pin-points of flame on miniature oil lamps. In the gloom they made out three figures stretched out on palliasses. One was a youth about twenty, very pale, his eyes gleaming in a face darkened by stubble, sweat standing out on his head, with one leg heavily bandaged in stained rags. It was he who was moaning. The other two were children, asleep, but obviously in high fever. There was a smell of stale vomit and something else too—not unlike putrid meat. Their guide stooped over the youth and wiped his brow with a cloth before cradling him in her left arm and offering him water from a wooden cup. She straightened and smiled at Claire.

'Ilatch,' she said, and pointed at her. 'Ilatch.'

Claire had bought more of the pills Booker had pre-scribed for her three days before in Ankara, and she recognized the Turkish word for 'medicine'.

In the early evening, as the valley slowly darkened, the whole clan gathered again to eat goatmeat stew and yog-hurt. Overcome with fatigue and excitement Claire had moved away from the fires—the smell of woodsmoke had set her eyes watering again—and had made her way up the slope to her rock where she sat, trying to order the confused impressions of the day. A figure followed her up, and as he drew near she recognized Robin.

'Hi,' he called. 'Do you mind if I join you?'

'Of course not.' She made room for him, and he sat beside her in silence for a while, letting the tranquillity of dusk flood over his intrusion.

'How do you feel about it all, now?' he asked at last.

'It's all really rather marvellous. Yes it is. Whatever we've missed by not going on, I'm glad I've had this.'

87

'Good.'

Stringed instruments, between guitars and mandolins in tone, joined the pipe and drum.

'How long do we stay?'

'That,' said Robin, 'is a matter of some controversy.'

'Oh? Why?'

'Well, Jack wants to move on. But Booker wants to stay at least a week to study the effects of the Panmycin. There's another complication too. Barzani says they must start the autumn migration in a day or two, down to Diyarbekir plain for the winter. So if we stay we'll be moving with them. Which might be rather interesting.'

'Why does Jack want to move so soon?'

'He's worried the Turks might miss us, and come looking.'

'He might be right.' She shivered.

'Cold?'

'A bit.'

'Let's go back then.'

As they walked down the slope, now almost completely dark, Claire stumbled and Robin reached out a hand to hold hers. He held on for a moment longer than necessary, and she gently released herself. Another thought returned to her.

'Where are these poisoned wells? You can't poison a glacier.'

'Down in the plains—where they go in winter. I don't think this clan has actually been hit by them yet. But there are some very sick people here.'

'We saw three of them. A boy with a bad leg and two feverish children—they could have measles or something.'

'I know. Booker's going to treat them. The boy is Barzani's nephew. He had a broken leg which didn't set properly and so they broke it again. He's probably got gangrene. The children probably do have some childish ailment. Booker's not sure yet. He'll treat all three tomorrow.'

In the morning Donna and Claire went with Booker to the tent where the sick Kurds were. It was the first time Claire had seen Booker as a doctor and the change was marked. The black man lost or restrained most of his exuberance. He worked with sureness but great gentleness taking their temperatures and pulses, softly crooning to the children with wordless soothing sounds that resembled the early morning rumblings of pigeons.

He moved on to the youth.

'This will be nasty,' he said, and his teeth flashed in the heavy darkness. Claire turned her head away as Booker began to unwind the bandages. The putrid stench became almost unbearable. Booker worked on, his long fingers busy and sure. At last he stood up.

'O.K., we'll give them a shot each.' There was a note, not of unsureness in his voice, but as if he was taking a step, after careful consideration, into the unknown.

Claire murmured to Donna. 'Why didn't he give them any yesterday?'

'He wanted to be sure of his diagnosis.'

The lamplight glinted on the syringe as Booker held it up. A drop of spurted fluid fell on Claire's hand and she absently wiped it on her smock. One of the children whimpered and then squawked, and Barzani, who was standing behind them, laughed deeply. Everyone relaxed and smiled, the Kurds began to chatter and Booker talked to Barzani in French as he packed his bag and followed the chief's son blinking out into the light.

Jack Dealer was waiting for them, arms folded, smoking. He slung the half-finished cigarette away and turned to face them.

'All right, we can go now. I mean it's done, so, O.K., we can go.'

Booker wiped his brow on a big yellow handkerchief, and set his bag down. 'You go, Jack,' he said.

'Oh, come on Booker. They've got the stuff and they know how to use it. I've been packing up, so let's hit the trail.'

Booker sank to his haunches and smiled up at the American, but he looked as immovable as one of the boulders on the hillside.

'You go Jack. Give me a week, and I'll be ready to follow you. Take the others, and leave me a van if you like. Or just leave me. I'll make out.'

'Hell Booker I might just do that.' Dealer turned on his heel, but only out of the wind to light another cigarette. 'Booker, what is this? Tell Jack.'

'Jack, go fuck yourself.'

'O.K. If you won't tell me, maybe the others will.' He turned to Robin, but it was Claire who spoke, although she blushed as she did.

'Booker's a doctor. He's taken on three patients, that's all.'

Booker unfolded himself and reached out to smack Claire's behind.

'Well done, chicken. That's not quite it, but it'll do for Yogi Bear here. The fact is this Panmycin isn't checked right out yet. I'm staying till I see there are no allergies or reactions, get it?'

Jack's face turned purple and his fists knotted. 'Christ. We risk ten years or more in Ankara jail, and this black boy has to play at ... at being Schweitzer!'

This time he did go, and after a moment's hesitation Robin followed him, trotting across the grass to catch him up, and then throwing his arm round Jack's shoulder.

Claire turned back to Booker to find him talking earnestly with Barzani. Her French, strictly grammar school, could cope with Racine but not this fast, idiomatic Middle Eastern patois.

'What was all that about?' asked Donna.

'They want to move tomorrow,' said Booker. 'Apparently they have already delayed their winter migration four days waiting for us. I'll have to stay with them until they get to the winter pasture. That boy shouldn't be moved. I've said we'll take him in one of the vans.'

'For Christ's sake, how long is all this going to take?' Donna's impatience had a note of hysteria in it.

'About a week, honey baby, just a week—as long as the weather holds. We go down into the plain, cross the Diyarbekir road; and about twenty miles on they've got a valley —a nice spot it sounds like. Now honey keep your cool. There's no danger. Only when we cross the main road maybe.'

'A week! And some of it in open country with a main road to cross! That's just fine. You tell Jack. You just tell Jack.'

CHAPTER III

Claire kept away from the expedition for the rest of the day. Something seemed to have cracked: the rather strained, artificial camaraderie had gone—gone with the illusion that they were going to Bangladesh. Idly she wondered how much each of the others had known, but she was not much bothered to find out: she felt they had all, except perhaps Donna, been in it from the start, and just at the moment she was glad to feel separate, apart from them.

She wandered down to the riverside and watched the women beating out clothes with stones; she played with some of the smaller children who were less shy now—indeed they were ready to giggle at her strangeness. She got bored with them and walked further up the valley to where the men on their ponies were rounding up the herds. There were black, shaggy goats, rather vicious; some smaller ones, finer looking, which she thought might be Angora; and, most numerous of all, fat-tailed sheep which were larger than most English sheep and had tails that spread into a flat plate which bounced comically behind them. Fierce looking dogs with spiked collars chivvied and snarled round them—on her own she was rather frightened of the dogs.

She started at the sound of small hooves on the grass behind her and the chink of harness. Barzani was in working clothes now—plain serge, an embroidered but shabby waistcoat, leather gaiters, yet he still carried himself with a dignity that made the flat cap he wore all the more incongruous. He touched his long whip to the peak and swung down to the ground beside her. They talked in French and soon she found she could follow him without too much difficulty.

'Pardon me, but do not go further from the camp: it is dangerous.'

'Dangerous?'

'There are wolves and bears in the mountains. They keep away in the summer, but some of them will follow us down. They know we are moving.'

He thanked her for coming, for bringing the Panmycin. 'Many of us are ill in winter. It is a bad time. Even on the plain there are three or four months of snow, and temperatures of minus thirty-five degrees at night. Every year several children die of pneumonia, and the old people have rheumatism. Now we have enough medicines for many years, for many winters.'

'But I thought I understood you were giving it to all the Kurds; to help you all ... for freedom.'

He laughed and patted his pony's neck as it stirred at the sound.

'For freedom, yes. If our clan can increase in numbers perhaps we shall be able to weave and spin enough to get money to build a village at our winter pasture, and only the young men will have to come up here in the summer. The government have said they would build us a village, but only if we become farmers, and grow crops on the plain. That we can't do. We are herdsmen. But the tents make a hard life: the Panmycin will help us, and perhaps one day we shall have a village which we have built and yet still be sheep farmers. That is our dream.'

Claire was confused. But her French was too slow to question him.

'In the meantime my nephew will get better, and that is good.'

He repeated his warning and cantered back to his work.

Claire did not know what to think. Had they really come all this way, had CHAP put up all that money, had they risked imprisonment to give a community of less than a hundred souls ten thousand doses of a new antibiotic? She couldn't believe it, but she was reluctant to disbelieve Barzani. Rarely had a man so impressed her: his directness, his dignity, the love and respect his people had for him, all made her sure that he was speaking the truth as he knew it. In the end she shrugged the questions away— what did it matter? No doubt when he realized how much Panmycin he had he would pass some on. It would be used by people who needed it and for whom even aspirin was a novelty. For the rest, well it had been an interesting trip, no harm would come of it if they got out of Turkey without being arrested again, and it had been an experience, even if not the experience she had expected.

Next morning the clan moved. It took from dawn to ten o'clock to clear the site. The noise was impressive: various songs or chants accompanied each activity; the dogs barked; bells chimed and harness jingled; horses whinnied; and dust began to billow from the dry, close-cropped turf. When the procession was assembled Sheikh Ibrahim raised an ebony staff and with a great shout they all moved. Then they stopped while Ibrahim was hoisted into a rough sort of sedan chair, and then they moved again, following the bank of the stream, down, out of the mountains. The older men led the way with the women, then came the Volkswagens, each carrying one of the sick, finally the flocks with Barzani, the able-bodied men, and the dogs.

'This stream,' said Robin, 'is a tributary of the Tigris.'

'Really?' Claire was impressed.

'Yes. Their winter pasture is near where it joins the Tigris. About half way between Diyarbekir and Siirt.'

But progress was very slow. It soon became obvious that not even air-cooled Volkswagens could continue long at two miles an hour. Robin pulled into the side and the others followed suit. Barzani came up with them and after some discussion it was decided that one of the boys would ride with Robin and point out the way ahead of the column. This meant that space was cramped on the front seat and Claire asked to be dropped amongst the women and children. Robin tried to argue, but he had been taciturn or irritable since the argument between Jack and Booker and Claire was in no mood to listen to him. He agreed in the end but only after he had made her promise to catch him up—he would never allow himself to be more than a mile ahead—as soon as she felt tired.

There was little danger of this: the pace was of the most casual stroll in the country—and what country! When she got bored she could stop and sit on a rock or climb a tree and watch the procession go by, and then scamper to the front again when the herds caught up; or she could run on ahead with some of the children and play hide and seek, throw fir cones, or swap language lessons. For the first two days they saw no sign of human life except when they crossed a barely discernible track; the weather remained fine, the mountains soared above them, the river chattered on. Claire deliberately shunned her companions and, for a time, began to believe in the illusion that she was part of the migration, was really living with the Kurds.

This pastoral dream could not survive the break in the weather on the third evening. During the afternoon the air became hot and heavy, and the birds no longer sang. Children began to cry, to act spitefully. Huge black clouds built up behind them and thunder rolled threateningly in the valleys they had left. Barzani rode by to the front, his face set and serious and then returned shouting at the women. Although it was only four o'clock the column halted, but even before the fires could be lit the rain came. A pony rider was sent on ahead to call back the vans and he disappeared behind a curtain of falling water as the clouds opened and lightning linked the peaks around them and the thunder let loose barrages of noise above.

Claire spent a wretched night in the vans with Robin and the youth who seemed to be little, if at all, better. The rain slid in sheets down the windows—to get out was to be instantly soaked—and the clan huddled under makeshift shelters, tents jury-rigged out of kilims and rugs which quickly ballooned with the weight of water and threatened to fall on the women and children beneath. Twice during the night Barzani came to discuss the situation with Robin, and Claire learned that the clan would move on the next day—however bad the weather: they dare not risk being trapped in the mountains by swollen rivers or impassable quagmires.

The next two days were hell. The rain did not stop though it varied between sharp, windy squalls, misty drizzle, and returning cloudbursts. Mud was everywhere— in the hair, down your back, plastered against your sides where you fell, in your shoes. The clan no longer looked like noble nomads: the weather reduced them to a dirty, hungry, miserable, cold rabble of refugees. Even the sheep and goats seemed to suffer. In spite of heavy duty tyres the vans stuck in the mud until they put on the chains. Claire began to appreciate Barzani's desire for something that would alleviate pneumonia and arthritis.

On the fifth day the valley broadened. Signs of cultivation, terraced slopes, appeared; they were on a definite track and movement, in spite of the mud, became easier, though the column was stretched out over nearly two miles by the narrowness of the way, beneath the gun-metal sky. At last they passed through two villages whose inhabitants eyed them with surly suspicion and even hatred. The few women about clutched their children to their rain-soaked skirts, and as they passed a teahouse they heard sounds of jeering from behind the steamed up windows. An old man made the sign to avert the evil eye. One of the villages had a militia post—the gendarme blinked at the sight of the vans and turned to his battered field telephone, the valley's only link with the outside world. But no one in the expedition was aware of this. They camped that night on the plain which is the wide valley of the Tigris.

At noon on the sixth day they crossed the main road between Diyarbekir and Siivas, and two miles further on the army were waiting for them.

They were entering a wide ravine which would eventually empty itself into the Tigris. About a mile or so on either side of them weird cliffs rose up a couple of hundred feet or more, eroded into layer cakes of rock and mud of differing ochreish hues. The track was bounded by shallow ditches and beyond these fields of stubble stretched away. The rain and mist still swept over and in front of them, almost veiling a bend in the track a quarter of a mile away. The three vans in their usual order were leading the procession, and immediately behind came Sheikh Ibrahim, shoulder high in his sedan chair.

Round the bend appeared a line of horsemen, twenty abreast across road and fields. Even at that distance and in those conditions Claire could see they were soldiers in khaki, helmeted, the five flankers at each end carrying lances, the rest with guns. The line, perfectly regular, was bearing down on them at a brisk trot.

What happened next was very confused and quick. Claire had barely time to clutch Robin's arm, before her attention was distracted by the sudden roar of a powerful engine increasing revs, followed by a crash. Over her shoulder she saw that Jack, who had seen the soldiers too, had tried to reverse his Volkswagen off the track, through the ditch and into the field. But he had misjudged the closeness of Booker and Donna, and his rear bumper had caught their wing, and then his momentum had carried him back until he was at right angles to the track. His powerful horn blared, his back wheels spun in the ditch throwing up sheets of watery mud, while Booker, unable to do anything else, shunted his vehicle into the space Jack had left. Jack wrenched his steering wheel to full lock and revved again, faster and faster, as the tyres continued to grind into the mud. Later he swore that he intended to wheel right off the track and on to the field, meaning to escape down the flank of the column, carrying the Panmycin out of reach of the soldiers. But suddenly the tyres gripped and threw the van, momentarily out of control, and in reverse on to the track, and into the centre of the group carrying Sheikh Ibrahim.

The roof caught one of the poles supporting the sedan, and the old man, like a limp black rag, was hurled out across the heads of his men to fall heavily on his neck in the mud. One of his guard, uninjured and still on his feet, drew a heavy revolver which he emptied into Jack's V.W. as it lurched off the road, through the ditch, and on to the field again. Claire heard the whine of a ricochet, passing over her as she thought, and two hundred yards away, still dim through the mist and rain, the soldiers halted. Then, in good order, they wheeled out to right and left, spreading out over the fields.

There was a moment's silence and Claire could hear the drumming of rain on the roof.

More screams, a thunder of hooves, and Barzani with about eight men swept up from the rear. He swung down from his saddle to land on his knees by his father. Claire saw him turning the old man over and then Barzani lifted his head to the rain and let loose an extraordinary cry, not a shout, or a scream, but something between the two. Then he too drew a revolver, remounted, and knives and

98

guns appeared in the hands of his followers. But, before they could move to attack the soldiers who they thought had killed Ibrahim there was a distant percussion, three seconds, and a heavy explosion tore the air fifty yards to the right. The seat rocked beneath Claire and a shower of light gravel and earth swept across the roof.

Robin plucked her out of the seat; he hurled her away from the van across the road and into the ditch; then he threw himself over her, pressing the side of her face into the mud and water. Around them the women and children were following suit; the men wrenched their ponies' heads round and galloped away, back to the flocks. Only Barzani remained standing by his pony, looking down at his father.

From their flank came the clatter of a machine gun, and bullets pocked across the track a few yards in front of Barzani. Slowly he spread his arms, palms out, in a gesture of resignation rather than defeat. Claire heard the clop of hooves again and ten mounted soldiers took form and substance in the mist ahead and came trotting towards them at the same disciplined pace they had been using before the first fatal shots had been fired. Booker joined Barzani and knelt over the body of the old man.

CHAPTER IV

Claire awoke on the third morning of this, her second spell in a Turkish prison, with none of the 'where-am-I' feeling. Too quickly the cramped cell in a partitioned nissen hut that she shared with Donna had become totally familiar: the white-washed walls, grubby with graffiti; the two cots with half inch mattresses; the small window with chicken wire stretched across it and its view of a rain-swept parade ground; the impossible toilet facilities and the food—sour gruel with grey bread—all added up to a misery that Claire had not known before, not even in Spain. No one spoke to them, no one seemed able to understand them. There had been no formalities, no trial, they did not know if the outside world had had news of them. They did not even know if the men were still nearby: as Donna said, for all they knew Booker, Robin, and Jack might have been taken away and shot.

And so Claire awoke slowly with the sick feeling in her stomach of being horribly lost. She did not dare move —the air she breathed was dank and she did not want to let it into the warm nest her body had created since dusk. She lay there almost weeping, conscious of the dirtiness that seemed to crawl over her skin, trying hard not to wonder what was to become of them, trying to think only of the immediate future, of getting through another day with Donna.

Donna was a problem. At first they had both been enormously relieved that their confinement was not solitary;

for the first evening they had tried to be brave, even joke about it. But this had been a failure. Donna had searched the graffiti for obscene drawings and when she found one she had commented on the absurd anatomy with a wild sort of near hysterical wit. Claire had not realized until then that sick humour could make one feel actually sick. The first full day had started well enough but then Donna had begun to worry about Booker; this had led her to tell Claire the most intimate details of her life with him; and finally to trying to get Claire to talk about her own experiences. This had led to a quarrel, almost a fight, and that ended with a chummy cuddle and a 'let's kiss and be friends' session on Donna's bed. This had been innocent enough, but Claire had been disturbed—there had been a wild excitement in the quarrel and an enervating warmth in their embraces. Such events would recur, and with more intensity, if they were so completely alone for many days more.

The second day had been a little better. Both had felt a sapping lassitude, and perhaps some shame about the day before. It had been colder and they had stayed in their thin quilts most of the time, talking in a desultory fashion, trying to find subjects of emotional neutrality—films they had seen, books they had read, word games. Donna had had stomach cramps and both of them had been seized with the fear of being ill, of getting dysentery.

'That grabs me,' she had said. 'Deliver a shipment of anti-cholera antibiotics to Kurds and then die of it in a Turkish brig.'

Now on the third day Claire lay awake, conscious of Donna's dark hair scattered over the pillow a yard away. If she stretched out she could stroke it. She shuddered and bit her lips at the thought. The distant sound of an engine distracted and relieved her, a steady explosive beat above the clatter—a helicopter. It was coming very close, overhead, the note changed, the beat slowed and stopped.

Unable to resist the first real event in two days Claire jumped out of bed to the window. Donna stirred.

'What is it?'

'A helicopter. Just landed.'

'Can you see it?'

Claire felt Donna's hand on her shoulder, the nesty warmth of a breast on her back, and that hair on her cheek. She could smell the musty odours of a newly awakened body.

By pressing closer to the corner of the window and to each other they could just see the long tail boom and the rear of the passenger section. Soldiers were standing on the far side of the boom, only visible from the waist down. Four pairs of civilian legs came down a ladder. There was a pause then the legs walked off away from them, out of sight, hidden by the body of the chopper.

'Shit,' breathed Donna in Claire's ear.

They separated and sat on their own beds, not quite facing each other since there was not room to do so. Claire's eyes began to run. Donna put a hand on her knee. 'O.K. honey, it may be O.K.,' she said. 'They were civilians, they may be here because of us. It gives us something to think about. But for God's sake don't start sniffing again.'

But the morning wore on with the established routine of gruel and ablutions unbroken. Donna amused herself adding to the graffiti, using the buckle of her belt. She scratched her name, and the date, Booker's name, a heart and arrow. Claire began to wonder what else she would add, when at last they heard steps, marching. A shout of command, locks turning, a young officer saluted.

'Please come with me,' he said.

They were led right away from the nissen hut to the largest building on the site. Outside the crescent and star hung limp in the watery sunshine, and white-helmeted soldiers snapped to attention as they climbed the steps. They were led into a long hall with a table and chairs at the far end in front of a regimental flag. Behind the table sat three men, one a soldier, and to their delight Robin, Jack, and Booker were there too. Donna flew down the room and into the black man's arms. Claire felt a tinge of personal envy, for the warmth of an uncomplicated embrace. Robin smiled as she sat down next to him, patted her hand and whispered, 'Are you all right?'

Her nod seemed to satisfy him.

The man facing them, a large almost fat man, with lined and pocked face and hanging wallets of flesh beneath his eyes and stubbly chin, cleared his throat raspingly.

'May I introduce myself? I am Alp Vural of the Special Branch. This is Brigadier Demirel whose hospitality you have been enjoying, and this is Colonel Nur Arslan of the Ankara police.'

Claire was pleased to see Nur again. He seemed to look more closely at her than at the others. Their eyes met and a hint of a smile warmed the policeman's dark eyes.

Alp went on to explain that they had committed a serious offence, that under the martial law in force they could be held without trial, or tried by a military tribunal. But men in the highest positions in the land had decided that their case was isolated, unlikely to be repeated, that they were foolish, ill-informed romantics, and that speedy deportation would be sufficient. They were to return as quickly as possible to the Greek frontier at Ipsala.

'The military are handing you over to the department of my colleague Nur Arslan,' he concluded drily. 'His department has responsibility for all criminal cases involving aliens. It will be his job to see that you reach Ipsala quickly and—er—safely.'

Nur leant across the table and spoke very seriously. 'I am putting one of my men, Lieutenant Gökalp, in the vans with you, and he will remain with you until you reach Ipsala. He can speak English. He will report to me by phone each evening, and during the day if anything untoward happens. If you do anything against his advice or instructions, or try to lose him, you will be imprisoned.'

There remained a few formalities: they were required to sign receipts for their property; Nur and the Brigadier exchanged papers; an agreed statement to the press was read out, and photographers were allowed to take their pictures. Through all this Claire felt as if she could explode with happiness and when they were at last in the V.W. she threw her arms round Robin and kissed him. To her disappointment he did not seem to share her mood —in fact he was as glum as he had ever been, but before he had time to answer or evade her questions a young man slipped under the guard post boom and raced up to them waving a piece of paper which he managed to thrust into Robin's lap before the soldiers caught him and hustled him back to the guard house.

Robin glanced at the paper. 'It's from Barzani,' he said. 'I must show it to Booker.'

He jumped to the ground and raced to the back of the tiny convoy. Jack and Lieutenant Gökalp, an ineffectual-looking young man, joined them. In the excitement it did not dawn on Claire that he was the man who had taken that photograph of her in Alexandropolis. A soldier was sent to the big building and Nur and Alp came hurrying out. Claire climbed out and hovered on the edge of the group, behind Donna.

'What is it? What's it all about?'

'A note from Barzani. His nephew, the one Booker gave Panmycin to, is very, very ill. He's worried about the others who were treated, the children.'

An argument had broken out. Suddenly Booker rolled his eyes to heaven so that the whites shone in his dark face, shouted an obscenity, and then, in the silence, spoke loudly, fiercely, but with control.

'O.K. Now listen good. This is where I come clean, but I'll have to simplify. I am employed by the General Drug Company. They sent me on this expedition and they put up some of the money. They have invested millions in Panmycin. They have competitors and they have to get Panmycin on the market ahead of them. I have been doing lab trials on the stuff for eighteen months but it's never been tried this side of the Iron Curtain in the field. Now, it's not for G.D.C. I'm speaking now but for those innocents I fed the stuff to. You know what side effects drugs can have: allergies, thalidomide, that scene. Those people need an expert in Panmycin, and I'm the only expert this side of Sofia. If you don't let me back to those people you can all be murderers. Dig this, Alp bey, and you Dealer and Bury: this is people now, not games for politicians. You understand that, Colonel Nur, sir. So we cool it, and get to those Kurds just as quick as we can, right? Or who knocks me on the head to stop me?'

'I might just do that,' said Dealer, his face mulberry again.

'Cool it—you heard me. Listen Jack, you're not the boss now. Colonel Nur's the man. You, we, are just going to do what the man says.'

Nur turned to Alp. 'Come with me. Doctor Jones, you come too. The rest stay here.'

They went back to the building and Jack began to swear quietly. Donna turned on him.

'For Christ's sake Jack. If they let us go back to the Kurds what does it matter? We came to do them some good, didn't we?'

'Listen rich girl. We're in a heap of trouble, up to here, right in it. Somehow we get off a real jail rap, we can blow; we came unstuck, but they let us walk right away, and now you and that do-good nigger are putting us right back where we started.'

'I don't see that it matters if Colonel Nur lets us go,' said Claire.

'Jesus I know what's gotten into him,' cried Donna. 'He ran down the Sheikh and killed him when we were attacked. He's scared shitless that Barzani will put a knife in him.'

'You nigger-loving bitch...'

Dealer might have hit her, but Robin pushed in, white with anxiety. 'Stop it. Now. Do you hear? Claire's right. If Nur lets us go, we go, if he doesn't we don't...'

A soldier came and spoke to Gökalp who then led them back to the long room. Nur and Alp were behind the long table, Booker stood near them, looking fairly pleased. Alp was angry. Nur spoke quietly.

'You will return to the Kurds for one night only. A squadron of motorized cavalry will go with you. If Doctor Jones thinks it is necessary a medical team will be flown out from Ankara and will reach the Kurds shortly after you have left. That is all.'

About two hours before nightfall they reached the black tents on a hillside about five miles from where the river they had followed joined the Tigris. It seemed a pleasant spot, not spectacular like the summer pasture, but sheltered. Down by the river poplars grew, still with a few yellow leaves shimmering above the mistiness, and there were fields of stubble between the river and the hills. Already the Kurds' flocks were scattered over the down-like slopes: the grazing looked poor, dry, brown, thistly, compared with the lushness of the mountains. But there was a golden, autumnal light over the scene and as their convoy, augmented by six army jeeps, halted about fifty yards from the nearest tent Claire could hear the goat bells and smell again the charcoal fires.

Their welcome was cool. As they climbed out of the

vans Barzani came to meet them. He wore the silver-edged black gown Sheikh Ibrahim had worn and carried the old man's black staff. He looked older, walked with a more measured pace, and Claire thought his eyes looked larger, brighter in the new shadows and hollows in his face. He spoke in French to Booker only.

'You needn't have come. My nephew died two hours ago. It would perhaps be better if you went on your way.'

'I should like to see the body.'

'Why? The women are washing him.'

'I must see the body. The others who had the medicine might be in danger. Your letter suggested this. I must see if the medicine made him more ill, perhaps killed him.'

'The others are better. His leg killed him. The poison spread to the rest of his body, no medicine could save him.'

'Sheikh Barzani, I must see the body.'

Barzani shrugged. 'Very well.'

He turned and Booker followed, carrying his black case.

'He can't go up there alone,' Donna cried.

Hesitantly the rest followed, accompanied by Lieutenant Gökalp who had ridden with Dealer. Claire heard steps and puffing behind her—Alp Vural. He looked very grim when they told him the youth had died. Claire wondered why he was there.

Barzani led them to the chief's tent. Beneath the large black awnings a group of women were huddled round a low bed of cushions and rugs. A dull, low chant filled the air. There were basins and ewers in silver and copper. As the group parted Claire could see the corpse. Only her grandmother's had she seen before laid out in a chapel of rest, and she turned away with shock and nausea, but soon felt compelled to look again.

The youth, naked save for a cloth over his groin and a scarf round his jaw, was flat on his back, but there was no beauty or serenity in the figure. The bad leg was swollen, purple, black, green, with streaks of blood and raw flesh. There were ugly blotches, red and purple, over most of his body. The joints of his fingers were heavily swollen and the bruised flesh covered the cuticles of his nails. His face too looked black and bruised. Booker knelt by him and his quick thin fingers fluttered over the body, probing, pinching, searching. Dealer stood behind him.

'Septicaemia from the leg and allergy?' he suggested.

The frown of concentration deepened on Booker's face. 'Maybe.'

He looked up for Barzani and found him. 'Tell me how he was since we left.'

Barzani questioned the women, they answered, he turned back to Booker and spoke with care. Claire could follow most of what he said.

'The day after you had gone, he was better, but still very weak. We gave him more of the medicine from the tray you gave us on the morning we left the mountains. The next day the fever came back only worse. He could not keep still. All yesterday he got worse, he threw himself about even though the leg hurt. He screamed. We gave more medicine. Before dawn his breathing became bad and he spat blood. I sent you my message. He went into a coma shortly after the sun had risen. He died.'

Booker opened out his case and took out slides, swabs, small glass dishes with tight lids. The women moved forward with a murmur of protest, but Barzini raised a hand and they held back. At last Booker straightened.

'O.K., I'll have to do some work on these. But I should be through by morning.' He poured water from one of the ewers into a bowl, added disinfectant, and scrubbed his hands. Then he packed away his gear. 'One thing Barzani. I'd like the tray of medicine you still have. If I find it's clear I'll let you have it back if the police don't object.'

Barzani led them back to the Volkswagens. As dusk fell they unpacked their tubular frame tents for the only time on the trip, because Booker had said he would need the van to work in, and, just that once, Donna and Claire actually prepared a meal—tinned beans and sausages—over the gaz stoves. Between them and the Kurds the soldiers bivouacked more primitively but with greater efficiency. Alp Vural was nowhere to be seen.

They ate in silence. A heavy dew was falling and as they cleared away Robin suggested that they should get into the tents. Booker looked up. 'Not me, man. I got work to do.'

'Can we help?'

'Not if you're not certificated as a lab technician in morbid pathology.'

'Ah, come on,' said Dealer, 'his leg went putrid. There was putrefaction before we got there. Maybe he was allergic too. Some people always are.'

'Why did he spit blood, Booker?' asked Donna.

'He died, actually died, of bronchopneumonia. That need be no great surprise, in the state he was in and the cold too. Now keep Dealer off my back. He knows I got my job to do, and not much time for it either!'

He stood up and moved off to his V.W. Carefully he unpacked everything from the back and lifted the roof so that he could stand inside. He opened the gaz stove and set up the table on which he laid out his travelling laboratory. He fixed up a bright hurricane lamp and got a gaz burner going low for heat. Claire went into her tent, snuggled into her sleeping bag, but left the flap open so she could watch him working. He made a striking figure, dramatically lit as he was. She could hear the chink of glass and metal, the hiss of the burners, and occasionally he hummed to himself. After an hour or so Donna appeared beside him.

'Okay, honey?'

'Fine, white girl.'

'Would you like something?'

'Coffee? Put some in a flask and then you get some sleep.'

Claire stirred. 'Hi,' she called. 'Get me some too.'

'Okay.'

Claire did not drink much, though it was hot, milky, and sweet. Heaviness settled on her, fatigue rushed up over her, and her eyes began to fall. As sleep overcame her she was aware, she remembered later, of a change in Booker's activity. He was writing more urgently, writing up notes.

Shortly after dawn Donna found him, a hundred yards up the hillside, dead, from knife wounds.

CHAPTER V

Two men sat in a large black car ten miles away on the main road. An army jeep came up the valley towards them, spewing dust behind it, so quickly does the rain seep away through the meagre soil. Alp Vural climbed down and joined Nur and Mr Mundham in the car. To Nur Mr Mundham was now Paul; Alp also used the first name—somewhat to Paul Mundham's distaste. He did not like this old policeman whose frame was crumbling with tobacco and alcohol and who seemed to have the power to keep his daughter from him, to keep her even from the reach of the law. Nur and Paul were in the front. Alp let his mass collapse on to the worn upholstery behind them. He was having difficulty with his breathing, but he immediately lit a cigarette and coughed on it.

'This is no life for me, being lumped across Anatolia in jeeps. All right Paul, your daughter's quite safe. She's in no danger. She's even in quite good spirits. Got something useful to do, you see, mothering the American girl.'

'Donna Liss has taken it badly, then?' asked Nur.

Alp shrugged. 'In a way. Couldn't get her off the body. She lay on it and got blood all over herself. She screamed a lot.'

He shuddered at the memory and picked a shred of tobacco off his moist underlip. 'The odd thing was she seemed more angry than grieved. Very angry. At last she stopped screaming and crying and started swearing. Very coldly, quietly, you know? I've never heard such language.

I know English well and I read American "policiers", so I knew the words—but I've never heard them before. Then she said she would kill the murderer and—er—mutilate his body. Then she let Paul's daughter take her away and the last I saw they were drinking coffee.'

Paul listened to this with mounting impatience touched with fear.

'Alp bey,' he had learnt the correct form of address, 'I don't see how you can say my daughter is safe. There is a killer down there.'

'And ten policemen and nearly forty soldiers.'

'The soldiers were there last night.'

Alp shrugged again, tossed his cigarette out of the window and lit another one. 'Nobody wants to kill Claire,' he said. 'She's a nice girl. Anyway they'll be clear of the Kurds by midday. I want them at least in Diyarbekir by night-fall. They'll be in Istanbul in three days and then it'll all be over.'

'Er it won't do.' Claire's father moved awkwardly on the seat. He wished he could face Alp properly, even stand —stand up to him. 'I really must insist you hand my daughter over to me. If you do not I shall go to the British Consul in Ankara and, if need be, the press.' He had overcome his reserve and he continued more firmly and quietly. 'I gather Colonel Nur must do as you say, but I am under no compulsion. You are virtually kidnapping my daughter and I insist she is restored to me.'

Alp laid a restraining paw on Mr Mundham's shoulder. The nails were cracked and dirty. 'Mr Mundham, you have my sympathy, but please do not talk of kidnapping. That is what the other side do.' He coughed heavily, opened the door an inch or two, and spat phlegm into the dust. 'You are right, Nur is doing as he is told. He does not do so usually. The local police are as well. They have a murdered body on their hands and, believe me Paul bey, that is as serious in our country as it is in yours. Yet they will let the expedition go on. They will pretend to believe a Kurd killed Doctor Jones; they will pursue their enquiries for some time after we have all moved on, and then drop them for lack of evidence. Colonel Nur knows why I am able to arrange these things. I have here,' he touched his jacket and smiled, 'authority from the Minister of the Interior to do just as I please until this business is finished. Do I make myself clear? You will not go to the press or your consulate until I let you. And it will be easier for you, and you may be of more use to your daughter if you do not try. There, I am sorry, but that's how it is. Now let us see this through as well as we can.'

There was a moment's silence then Paul Mundham opened his door and walked quietly away from the car. The two policemen watched him. For a time he stood by the roadside, staring down the valley. He kicked a stone, lit a Woodbine and smoked it through. Then he turned back towards them. His face looked paler but he still stood very straight.

'Very well. Just as you say,' he grunted, and let himself into the car again. 'But you will continue to let me stay as near to Claire as I can.'

Alp spread his palms.

'Of course,' he said.

A police doctor gave Donna a sedative. As soon as he had gone she cursed him, and announced that what he had given her was shit, junior aspirin, no more.

'If he wants to knock me out, he can have me out.' She rummaged about in her baggage and before Claire could stop her she had taken three more capsules of her own. Claire was terrified. She wondered how they would react with what the doctor had given her, if Donna had over-dosed herself.

'Don't bug me, little English girl. I know pills. Believe

me, I know pills. And don't worry—this won't be a bad trip, I won't get high or flip out. It'll just be night-time for me for ten or twelve hours ... you may have to get me carried upstairs if we ever get ... get to ... just sleep, is all little girl.'

She began to moan and sway. Claire got her into the back of the van and managed to roll her on to a sleeping bag and cover her with another one before her eyelids fluttered and she slept.

Slowly, like sleep-walkers themselves, Robin, Jack, and Claire dismantled their tents. Lieutenant Gökalp had told them that they were to drive on as soon as statements had been taken, and they had been too shocked to wonder why.

The question arose—who travelled with whom, who drove. Claire looked at Robin and then at Jack. Neither had shaved, neither had said much to her; both looked shifty, disturbed, they would not meet her eyes. She did not want to travel with either.

'I'm going with Donna,' she said firmly.

Robin tried to protest but Claire insisted.

'Lieutenant Gökalp can come with us and drive. You can take the other two.'

And so it was arranged.

An army ambulance drove off with Booker's body. A soldier came with a large red handkerchief knotted to hold the things in it. There was a pocket notebook too. Personal effects. Claire took them and put them on the dashboard shelf for Donna when she awoke.

They were about ready to go. Claire stood outside while Robin fussed around the tyres, and checked the oil, and so on. The valley seemed larger, emptier, as though they had already gone. The thin drizzle was falling again from a flat, featureless ceiling of cloud. The vans and police cars were scattered around like lifeless alien lumps, the wreckage of a spaceship from another planet. The soldiers too were now listless, huddled under glistening capes, smoking. Only the tents of the Kurds looked real, melting into the hillside; wisps of smoke rose from the fires—they were already snug for the winter, forgetting the transients who had intruded. Claire felt they had a propriety in their lives, a respect for the seasons out of which had grown a respect for each other that all those immediately around her lacked.

As she watched black figures detached themselves from the black tents; Barzani and two elders walked up the track, past the soldiers, towards the vans. No one tried to stop them.

Barzani halted in front of her, looked around, and then into the Volkswagen.

'The American girl is asleep,' he said. 'That is best. But I had something to say to her.'

Claire struggled with her French.

'You can tell me.'

'Very well, say this. Her man was a good man. Tell her my people neither wished him harm nor did him harm.'

He salaamed and turned away. Claire's tears mingled with the rain.

CHAPTER VI

Travelling east Claire's appreciation of the country had been superficial—places on the way to somewhere else—though she had enjoyed the emptiness of the steppe after the confusion of Istanbul. But on the way the sun had shone. Now the long, interminably long road stretched across the featureless plateau under a blank sky or circled glistening rocks beneath weeping pines while the images of horror mixed behind her eyes. Lieutenant Gökalp beside her hardly talked at all—he seemed frightened of driving at first and was clumsy with the unusual gears—at any rate he gave all his attention to the road and to keeping up with Robin. Behind Claire Donna snored heavily and occasionally moaned.

For the first night they stopped at Malatya. Donna was just awake enough to be helped rather than carried to the dingy, bare hotel room. There were beds like the ones in their army cell, and the same terrazzo floor, a scrap of carpet, a locker, a cupboard, and that was about it. Claire asked if some soup could be brought up to them and Gökalp arranged it: she still felt almost aversion at the thought of talking to Robin or Jack. The soup was oily with a half-poached egg floating in it and it was tepid too. Donna would not eat any but demanded her pills. They were in the car.

Claire went out into the street. A large black car was parked about a hundred yards behind. She thought she saw a hand wave, but it was almost dark, and the street badly lit; she thought nothing of it and went back in. She met Gökalp in the foyer. He was angry that she had gone, even to the street without telling him.

'I shall tell Colonel Nur Arslan if you do it again.'

She was irritated. He was like an officious prefect. She was dimly aware that there was something familiar about him, but she could not yet place it.

Donna sat up in bed with Claire's arm round her shoulders and took three more capsules and a drink of water from a bottle with a foil cap that had been left on the locker.

'Don't go,' she said, clutching Claire's wrist.

'I'm just settling your pillows, I'm not going.'

'Talk to me until I go to sleep.'

What was there to say?

'A soldier brought Booker's things. You know, from his pockets. I've got them for you.'

Donna gave a long sighing shudder.

'I don't want them. I don't want to see them. Throw them away before I can see them.'

Claire wondered whether to tell her about Barzani but after this decided not to. Soon Donna slept again.

During the next day—which was much the same as the one before though soon they were truly on the plateau with no mountains or plains to break the monotony, just the dun plain and ochre hills fissured and tumbled by erosion and earthquake—during the day Claire gained more control over her thoughts. She began to question and reason.

On the face of it it seemed clear enough. They had been taking Panmycin to the Kurds, not out of charity but to use them as guinea-pigs, to try the stuff out 'in the field' Booker had said, for the General Drug Company whose employee he had been. They had been caught. And now deported or returned to the frontier. But one of the Kurds had died and Booker had been murdered. Obviously one should think that a Kurd had killed Booker and that his death was the tragic outcome of a sordid scheme, but Claire could not bring herself to accept that a Kurd had done it; she would have found it difficult to believe even without Barzani's parting message. Who then? Robin Bury or Jack Dealer? That was unthinkable. An outsider? But who? Why?

The idea of an outsider, a silent watcher, a killer, was very frightening. But the questions now rushed in: the Bulgarian frontier, the shots, had Booker been wounded by frontier guards? Or by someone else? And there were other puzzles that now seemed more sinister: the photographer at Alexandropolis, the conversation she had overheard at the Turkish frontier; the customs officer who insisted on having samples of Panmycin; Guevara's ghost —what had his name been? Genghiz; Nur's interrogation of her in Istanbul—he had been polite, but why had she been the only one to be questioned? Dimly Claire was becoming aware of another world: it was like a science fiction story with different planes of reality; it reminded her of childish fantasies that the life she was leading was really part of someone else's dream—it was like Kafka.

'Miss Mundham, are you all right?'

Gökalp's eyes were fixed on the tail of Bury's Volkswagen, his hands clenched on the wheel. Claire realized she had gasped or cried out.

'Yes, yes, I'm all right.'

She went on looking at him though. Black hair, short, but swept back, snub nose, thin silky moustache—rather a squirt: a bit like the slick set from the boys' High School, the ones who used Brylcreem and became estate agents or went into insurance, who asked you to the pictures and tried to put their hands up your skirt. She smiled. 'Brapingers' the giggling fifth form had called them. But not policemen. Surely they never ended up as policemen. And then suddenly she went cold and then hot with embarrassment—the photographer at Alexandropolis and Gökalp, were they not ... yes, she was sure they were the same. Why had a Turkish policeman taken their photographs even before they reached Turkey? Was he a policeman?

How did she know he or Alp or Colonel Nur were policemen? Even that the soldiers were soldiers? No, that was absurd. Only in Bond films did crooks have private armies with camps, and jeeps, and trench mortars, and machine guns. Nevertheless she couldn't be sure about Gökalp. She could not be sure about anything.

She wished she had said to Gökalp, 'Yes, I'm ill, I want to go to the lavatory,' and then when he stopped she could run, and run, and run across the plain to Barzani, to her father in Heathleigh.

Donna moaned. Claire twisted round. The American girl's face was waxy pale, her hair plastered across her cheeks and even in her open mouth. Her eyes stayed closed. Booker's things: Donna wanted them thrown away. Claire unfolded the handkerchief: an identity bracelet, a gold Tau cross on a chain, loose change in three currencies, a Parker gold pen, a credit card, a penknife. She opened the wallet and found paper currency, dollars mainly, and a small notebook—hardly bigger than a pocket diary. Nearly half the pages had been torn out. She remembered her last sight of Booker, working on specimens taken from the dead Kurd, making notes. The notes had gone ... who? ... why? The police, if they were police, they might have torn them out. Evidence. Evidence of what? Claire's head began to throb. There was too much; there was another world; there was some plot, some intrigue around her that brought death, blew up jeeps, stabbed in the stomach, something which could strike again. Claire wanted out.

Donna moaned and Claire wrapped the things up. She would not throw them away, that would be silly. She stuffed them to the bottom of her folk-weave bag.

As the light began to thicken they entered Kayseri, Cappodocian Caesarea. They had passed through on the way out, and Claire remembered that she had wanted to stop, to look around, see some of what the guide book mentioned. Now all she saw was a drab collection of low concrete buildings, shanty towns, brash apartments with dirty paint, streets cobbled and too wide, ruins—yes, but ruins that had no romance about them, ruins that were just broken buildings.

The black car was there, ahead of them this time, parked a hundred yards up from the hotel. But there are black cars everywhere.

That night Donna wanted to talk again.

'Barzani spoke to me before we left. He had a message for you. Do you want to hear what he said?—it was about Booker.'

'Go on.'

'He thanked us for what Booker had done. He said, he said . . . ,' Claire could feel tears coming, '. . . that Booker was a good man. And that no Kurd killed him.'

Donna stared ahead, her eyes huge and dark, the irises almost gone. She began to shake, then laugh, tearing at the sheet, throwing her head and hair around. Claire hit her and she subsided into sobs and then hiccups. At last she lay back and her eyelids drooped. She turned her face to Claire and her grip tightened on Claire's wrist and her nails sunk in.

'Either you,' she whispered, 'either you, Robin or Jack killed Booker. And when I know which I shall kill whichever killed . . . which . . . who.' Her fingers relaxed and she slept again.

Claire cried and dozed and woke again. The light was still on. It was only eleven o'clock, but she felt clearer, calmer, though cold.

'Dear Evelyn Home . . .' she murmured to herself. Then sat up straight. This would not do. She was being a fool.

Donna was ill, she needed attention. They were in danger. So, something practical should be done. She hurriedly pulled out the guide book. Kayseri to Ankara, only two hundred and ten miles, a good road. Ankara to Istanbul another three hundred. So surely they would stop the next night at Ankara, and, because the distance was short, they would be there before nightfall. She had only to walk Donna out of whatever hotel they were in and into a taxi and up to the British or American Consulate and the nightmare would be over.

The amplified muezzin was still howling his prayer to a grey dawn when Gökalp woke them.

'We leave in half an hour.'

Claire pulled open the door and caught him on the corridor.

'Why are we leaving so early?'

'We must get to Istanbul by nightfall.'

No stop at Ankara then. Well, no matter. There were consulates in Istanbul. The guide book said so.

An hour or so after by-passing Ankara the terrain and the weather improved. Reforestation had halted soil erosion, small rivers wound down valleys with a faintly Chinese aspect—heightened by the terraced rice fields—the road itself was magnificent, wide, well engineered and landscaped, climbing into the mountains. The Bolu Pass felt like the roof of the world—a wide valley with peaks glimmering in the distance and pasture like the Kurds' 'yayla'. Then they crossed the watershed and below them range after range of peaks and hills receded into a lilac haze over the distant sea of Marmora. They stopped at a roadside spring: the water, which gushed from a hole in a carved slab covered with glowing green moss, was almost icy, yet soft like the air they breathed. Claire could not help feeling a lightening of the heart and she smiled as she watched Robin ducking his mouth under the spout. He caught the smile, shook water from his hair and out of his eyes and smiled shyly back.

'Not long now,' he murmured.

'Not long?'

'Before it's all over.'

Her fears rushed back and her face crumpled as she turned away. He reached out a hand for her arm, but she brushed him away as she stumbled back to the car.

The road dropped steadily towards Europe and as it did the land became more fertile. Fields of vines flashed by, their foliage burnished like beaten gold by the afternoon sun. They passed wide-eaved barns hung with tobacco leaves, and they marvelled at the autumn richness of everything. In the village markets there were huge piles of peaches, apples, and melons—the water melons slashed open to reveal their pillar-box succulence—and even the donkeys and water buffalo looked fat after the penury of the plain. The landscape, especially as they got nearer the Marmora, had a look almost of Southern England about it—untidier perhaps but civilized, used, prosperous, and as the hills rounded out, the scale became human. It was somehow unlike other Mediterranean areas and Claire was beguiled into wondering why. She came to the conclusion that it was because the villages were on the floor of the valleys, not up on the hills: they were unfortified—a witness to six centuries of Ottoman peace.

At last they came to the sea and for miles the road wound along the northern coastline of the Gulf of Izmit, the long finger of the Marmora that points up into Asia. Gökalp became more animated. Apparently he knew these parts; to him they were paradise: banyos and lidos, cement factories and tiny industrial ports, marinas, hotels and nightclubs. His rather inane chatter woke Donna. She sat up, pushed her dank hair out of her eyes, and made salivating noises in her mouth.

'God, I'm thirsty.'

Claire handed her a water bottle.

'Where are we?'

'Getting near Istanbul.'

'Christ, why does everything have to be so filthy?'

This, if it was directed at the seaside township they were passing through, was not really fair. But she probably meant the inside of the van which was a mess of dust, papers, half-eaten food, and badly packed baggage.

'I'm hungry.'

Claire gave her some chocolate.

'You seem a bit better,' she ventured nervously.

'Yes, yes I am. Have I been a burden? I suppose I must have been. Well, you can stop worrying now. I shan't be any more trouble to you. Unless.'

Claire turned. Donna's face was no longer waxy—indeed there was high colour in her face and a frightening un-focused intensity in her gaze.

'Unless?'

'Unless you killed Booker.' Donna laughed playfully without hysteria. 'But you wouldn't do that would you chicken? You liked him; he liked you. He called you chicken. It was one of those other bastards.' She started, peered forward and then quickly back and then smiled with satisfaction. 'Yes, they're still with us. That's okay.' She stretched out again lying on her back, her head im-mediately behind Claire, staring up at the ceiling. Pre-sently she began to hum, a tuneless but plaintive sound. Her hands fidgeted, plucking at thread ends on the sleeping bag or weaving patterns in front of her face like a child playing cat's cradles but without string. Claire shivered as the sweat that had broken out in her armpits and between her breasts evaporated.

The road became a street, buildings closed round—

villas, shanties, shops, blocks. The road climbed along the side of a hill, sometimes on a crest. To the right was a huge cemetery—long brown grass and twisted gravestones, oddly phallic with their stylized stone turbans. Gökalp gestured to a square grey building, very large, about half a mile down to the left.

'Florence Nightingale's hospital,' he said. 'We are coming to Üsküdar—Scutari. That war we had you on our side. Always it should have been. No Gallipoli, Russia conquered, together with Germany we would have ruled the world.'

The road dropped and the Bosporus spread out in front of them: the most beautiful skyline in the world—the ancient walls, the Topkapi Palace with its cypresses, St Irene, St Sophia, and the Sultan Ahmet Mosque with its six minarets glowing in the evening sun across the opalescent water.

CHAPTER VII

The ferry dropped them in the heart of it at the Sirkedji landing stage beneath Topkapi in a wilderness of quays, railway lines, garbage, cobbled alleys, and huge buildings. Through this the convoy threaded its way to the Pamuk Palas, a stone-faced block but with none of the faded grandeur of the 'Galata' where they had stayed before. The foyer of the Pamuk had a sort of cracked and peeling décor from the thirties—a decayed imitation of the Strand Palace—but the rooms were little better than those of the hotels in Malatya and Kayseri; however the noise outside was very different. To Claire it seemed that it went on all night—car horns, the roar of heavy lorries, the steady rumble of a huge city. For a brief spell something like silence descended but even that was scarred by the high-pitched sliding note of the nightwatchmen's whistles as they patrolled the streets and signalled from block to block that all was well. Then the muezzins, and it all started again.

The morning found Claire exhausted. She felt stiff, her throat was dry, her eyes and nose seemed on fire, she felt drained of all physical energy. But her determination to get Donna and herself to one of the consulates was undiminished, and indeed had become an obsession.

They had their breakfast—the standard fare of grey bread, white cheese and tea was enlivened by thin cherry jam and black olives—and when they had finished Claire simply said, 'Let's go out.'

'Gökalp will stop us.'

'If he does, he does, but let's try.'

Donna shrugged. 'Okay, let's try.'

Gökalp was not in the corridor, nor in the foyer, nor in the street. But there was a taxi.

'Meshrutiyet Caddesi,' said Claire, giving the name of the street in which both consulates had their addresses.

'Whatever for?' said Donna. 'The Büyük Bazaar. I may be able to get what I want there.'

She was very firm about it and although it was only a short drive the cabby took his cue from her and dropped them opposite one of the western entrances to the Bazaar. It was an unsettling sort of day with a cold wind blowing down the Bosporus off the Black Sea sending high clouds scudding in front. Very bright but fitful sunshine lit the rainwashed city giving it a drama it did not need. Garbage and trash whirled away from the fruit markets, and the last poplar leaves span away from the trees in the park. Gigantic red banners, hung from the top storeys to the ground floor of the main university building in celebration of some national holiday, billowed and cracked as the shadows of their folds rippled across, turning scarlet to crimson to scarlet again.

The girls ducked into the huge bazaar—endless passages and alleys of shops beneath high vaulted roofs stretched away in every direction, and a crowd, as of lost souls, drifted endlessly and apparently aimlessly in all directions, pushing, shouting, buying, selling, arguing, haggling, spitting and shaking hands, but all reduced to incoherent babel by the echoing vaults above them.

'I had not thought death had undone so many,' murmured Claire, but Donna still had her own purpose in mind and she headed off into the maelstrom with Claire tagging behind.

The first alley seemed to be entirely devoted to plastic goods. There were washing-up bowls, bins, fly-swats, buckets, brushes, and all in plastic. Donna was not inter-

ested. She pushed on taking turnings quickly as she identified what each lane specialized in. Carpets she did not
want. Old coins and stamps held her interest for a moment,
Ottoman antiques fascinated her and she actually made it
into one or two shops where she nosed around lifting
copper ewers to see what they hid and running her eye over
the bric-à-brac.

'You want a nice camel saddle, very ornate, very authentic? Or this copper coffee set, very valuable from the
Dolmabahce Palace kitchens—see I have a certificate of
guarantee, only fifty dollars, or...'

'No, no, hell, no.'

'Donna, what do you want?'

'For Christ's sake, what do you think? A knife of course.'

'Whatever...?' Claire's blood froze as she realized what
for.

The proprietor smiled and took them to the door.

'First left. Second right. Goodbye, you're welcome,
goodbye.'

Donna began to trot, with Claire's protests unheeded
behind her. Claire almost lost her but she remembered
the directions and found her in the ironmongers' street
in a shop entirely devoted to knives—all modern, but of
every shape and variety. Donna rejected three kitchen
knives and a carving knife though they looked deadly
enough when one thought of a stomach, a neck, or a back
rather than onions, carrots or cooked meat.

'They're sharp on one edge only,' Donna explained. 'And
I'd like a sheath.'

Although this was said to Claire it was said patiently
and the shopkeeper seemed to understand. He took them
into an alcove where the walls were lined with sheath
knives. They were even more harmless than the kitchen
ware—boy scout knives, short, with tin handles, coloured
like bone or wood. Claire's brother had had one. You
couldn't have sharpened a pencil on it.

Then a show case caught Donna's eye and she almost pounced.

Four daggers—very simple—blades about nine inches long, double-edged, thin, very sharp; handles wound with twisted silver wire, simple egg-shaped pommels and flared quillons embossed in the centre with swastikas.

The attendant looked doubtful.

'Gestapo daggers. They are much collected.'

'How much?' Donna whispered.

'Forty dollars or twenty-five sterling. Turkish lira, much more.'

Donna plunged into her canvas bag.

'Ten, twenty, twenty-five, twenty-six and a quarter. Claire lend me your sterling.'

'I haven't got any, honest.' Then she remembered that she had dollars and her face betrayed her. Donna seized her bag and tipped it out on to the floor. Last to drop was Booker's handkerchief and pocket book. Crouched over them Donna lifted her wild head and the words came from a frenzied face.

'Two tens. Honey, I'm glad you didn't throw them away.'

With her dagger scabbarded and gift-wrapped at the bottom of her deep bag, Donna seemed drained of energy and purpose. Standing on the pavement outside the bazaar again she looked round with the proprietary air of the slightly mad and said, 'I want some coffee. Real coffee. Not the oriental sludge they serve out here.'

Claire kept her head. She fished out the guide book, found the street map of the city and spread it out on the paving stones; the wind whipped it and threw dust in their eyes. They twisted round so that their backs were to the wind and a little crowd of Turkish youths gathered behind them unable to believe their eyes or their luck. Claire smoothed the map and, putting her hand over the Hilton, indicated 'Wagons Lit Cook' on Istiklal Caddesi almost opposite Meshrutiyet.

'There's sure to be American coffee somewhere round there.'

'Okay. Get a taxi. I've got a headache.'

A boy whistled for a taxi, and was tipped magnanimously with the last of Booker's dollars; the youths cooed and whistled softly, and peered in through the windows until the old Buick pulled out into the traffic.

They cruised down the side of the Valence Aqueduct with its view of the Mosque of Suleiman the Magnificent at the end and turned left under the arches into Atatürk Bulvar; crossed Atatürk Bridge—the grey waters of the Golden Horn whipped beneath them into yellow spume by the wind—and climbed with the trolley buses up into Galata. They paid off the cab on the steps of Cook's. Across the way Meshrutiyet Caddesi right-angled back down the hill and on the elbow a high wall surrounded a garden and what looked like a not inconsiderable Italian Palace. But it was the Union Jack that flapped and snapped on the flagpole above the heavy iron gates. Claire's heart began to pound as she took Donna's arm and firmly pulled her across the road.

'Where are we going?'

'It looks nice down there. There's a hotel round the corner. I bet they'll have coffee.'

The traffic surged, hooted and cursed around them. The road dropped steeply away back towards the Horn and Donna almost slithered right against the gates.

'Oh, look,' cried Claire. 'The British Consulate.'

'Oh gee. How swell!'

'I'd like to go in.'

'Whatever for?'

'Oh, I don't know.' Claire improvised. 'Yes, I do. They'd get a message home for us. Tell my parents we're all right.'

'Honey, you need a post office. But you go in if you want. I'll wait here. Don't be long.'

'Come with me.'

'Why?'

'Please come with me.' Inspiration failed. 'Please.'

'Honey, what are you up to?' Paranoia glimmered in Donna's eyes.

'I think we ought. I know we ought. We ought to go and tell them everything. They'll see we're all right. They'll look after us properly...'

'Why, you scheming little bitch!' Donna turned and began to run up the street. Claire caught at the swinging bag and slipped, and was dragged for a yard, but she wouldn't let go. She began screaming.

'Help, help, I'm English, help me, please help!'

Donna kicked at her, missed, and came down on top of her. Her sharp finger nails darted at Claire's face and then fastened round her wrist, tearing at her grip on the bag. The siren of an ambulance wailed like a banshee up the hill behind them.

'Let go, let go you...' The American girl's language became unprintable.

'Please, Donna, please, please, please...'

A screech of brakes, strong hands fastened on their clothes, lifted them to their feet, and twisted arms crookedly, agonizingly into their backs. White coats, dark glasses, a whiff of garlic on a man's breath, and still kicking and screaming Claire was hustled behind Donna into the back of the ambulance. As she fell into the darkened interior the double door slammed behind her, and the vehicle shot forward, its siren howling again.

From a narrow bench between the two bunks a distantly remembered face smiled at them—the thin beard, the dark glasses, the black beret, not of Che Guevara, but of Genghiz.

Back in the sunny windswept street, tranquillity returned and, impassively and ineffectually, above the iron gates the Union Jack continued to flap.

PART IV : THE CITY

CHAPTER I

Though Nur and Mundham were much disturbed when Gökalp rang through to the Police Headquarters, which were only a block or so away from the Pamuk Palas, Alp maintained an irritating lack of concern. In fact, seated behind the desk in the same room he had used before, he seemed almost smug. He was sure he said, that trained observers of the Third Section would have seen the girls leave, and tailed them, and would be on hand should anything untoward happen. In the meantime a walk and a bit of sightseeing would do the girls good. And with that Colonel Nur and Mr Mundham had to be satisfied.

The minutes ticked by and Nur and Paul smoked restlessly and drank tea while Alp worked in a desultory way. A thought took root in Nur's mind, grew and bore fruit.

'Alp bey,' he said at last, 'this isn't one of your games, is it?'

'Games, my friend?'

'It could be that you hope the other side will also follow the girls, and give themselves away to your men.' He spoke quietly but Alp could hear the threat, foresee the outburst of Nur's tiresomely righteous wrath if he admitted any such thing. And yet it was difficult to deny: Alp was an opportunist—it had occurred to him that Gökalp would not be able to keep an eye on all four at once, and he had warned his men of the possibility that the guerrillas would be watching the foreigners.

'My friend, there are some questions it is silly to ask.

Now look, there is a Hadji Bekir on the corner of the street. Let me send for some Turkish Delight or *petits fours*. I am sure Paul bey would like to sample the real thing...'

The telephone rang.

Alp listened, shouted and cursed. Paul Mundham, who had quite fancied the idea of Turkish Delight, listened with growing alarm. At last the receiver was replaced.

'Your men have lost them,' said Nur coldly.

'In the covered Bazaar,' Alp tried to reconstruct an atmosphere of calm. 'It is an easy place for it to happen. All the exits are now being watched. Or will be in five minutes.'

'How long ago were they lost?'

'Perhaps ten minutes, not more.'

'So, they have had a quarter of an hour to leave the market and go anywhere they like in the whole city.'

Paul cleared his throat. 'Um, what are we going to do now then?'

Alp's shoulders rose again, but this time with less complacence. 'Wait. What else? There is really no cause for alarm. I am sure they will be back in the hotel soon. Gökalp will ring as soon as they are. Now, please let me send to Hadji Bekir and we can save some coffee too.'

Nur touched his chest in the gesture of polite refusal.

'Er, no, not just at the moment, thank you,' murmured Mr Mundham.

The next two hours were the worst Mr Mundham had yet experienced, and though there was far worse to come, he always remembered the sheer frustration, the total helplessness of that time. So far he had borne up well. Although nearly sixty he had kept himself fairly fit by attending a country dance club. He was used to stress and overwork and the long hours of travel and uncertainty had not yet drained him. He had a lively, curious mind, and the interest of being in a foreign country, even under such circumstances, had distracted him. There had been moments when he had caught himself almost enjoying it all. The company of Nur Arslan too had been more than a comfort. Paul liked the Colonel, got on well with him, felt confident that if there was any man in Turkey who could get them out, Nur was that man. That, perhaps, made this wait all the more difficult to bear, for Nur was obviously very worried.

At the end of the first hour Nur exploded.

'This won't do, Alp bey. You have acted with gross irresponsibility. I insist you alert the City Police Forces and get those girls found.'

Alp's fists clenched on the desk in front of him, and slowly relaxed. He picked up a ball point pen and stabbed the air.

'Probably they are at the hairdressers or having coffee at the Hilton.' His voice became icy. 'But perhaps the guerrillas have got them. In which case, just one policeman has to see them in a car, or on the ferry, or being hustled along the street, and blow his whistle, and...' The pen snapped in two between his fingers.

At midday the telephone rang again. Alp flicked a switch and Nur came closer to follow the conversation on the tiny extension speaker.

'Alp Vural speaking.'

'A call, sir. Do you want it traced?'

'Yes, but no further action. Put it through. Alp Vural here.'

'Ah, the Deputy Director himself.' The voice was soft but quick, with an underlying hint of maniac urgency. 'My name is Genghiz. All right? You know who you are talking to?'

Alp was breathing heavily, and Paul noticed sweat beads forming in the folds of skin on his face. Nur too seemed to be listening with a frightening intentness.

'Of course. Get on.'

'We have the girls. You know? The English and the American?'

'I know.'

'Good. Now naturally we wish to come to an arrangement for their safety. But the terms are a little complicated and so I should be grateful if we could meet and discuss them. Obviously there should be no possibility of misunderstanding between us: that could be tragic, so I do think it would be better if we met.'

'I'm listening.'

'Good. I suggest we meet in Aya Sofia. This afternoon at two o'clock.'

'Today's Monday. It's closed.'

'Precisely. Have it opened by one thirty and then cleared of all guards and staff. I want you, Robin Bury, and Jack Dealer with the Botulin XP3, no one else, entering the South Gate at two precisely. You will go to the Sweating Column and wait there. Now listen, Alp bey effendim. If there is one person, even the Curator himself, anywhere in the building, we shall not come, the deal will be off, and your two nice girls will be dead in the Bosporus by half-past two. And I know that is a risk you daren't take. Victims of kidnapping have died before but never so soon after their capture, and never without prolonged and publicized attempts from the authorities to rescue them.'

The phone clicked.

'What,' asked Nur, 'is Botulin XP3?'

'Panmycin?' suggested Alp.

The outer courtyard of Aya Sofia was almost completely sheltered from the wind, and was deserted apart from the pigeons whose wings racketed away as the Curator himself unlocked the doors of the public entrance from the outside, where he reluctantly remained.

Alp led the way; Robin and Jack followed carrying one

134

of the cases of Panmycin between them. Robin was confused and had been for days, too confused to take in the huge pile of domes and cubes and massive buttresses that climbed rather than soared up to the huge dome in the centre much like the foothills and lesser peaks surrounding a great mountain. Like Claire he had asked himself questions but he remained lost in uncertainties. He only knew that something had gone very wrong. The gift of Panmycin to the Turkish Army of Liberation as well as to the Kurds had always been to him the chief justification of the expedition but it had been no part of the plan that it should be taken as ransom for Claire Mundham, the girl he had promised himself he would take care of.

Their feet crunched on gravel as they passed the tombs and *turbes* of long dead sultans, and the ablutions fountain beneath the cypresses. The cliffs of stone closed round them and the shadow of the Baptistery struck cool across Robin's back. More gates creaked open and clanged shut and a long, wide gallery stretched darkly in front of them. Gold gleamed from a mosaic above their heads but no one stopped to look at it. The wall to the right was pierced by huge gateways through which Robin glimpsed the enormous expanse of the nave. The fourth and largest gate was open; they wheeled through it and stood beneath the cupola.

The echoes of their footsteps faded away into a silence broken only by the chirp of a lost sparrow and the ghostly flutter of its unseen wings. The sombre magnificence of the building which had stood for centuries as the largest in the world halted their progress and fleetingly emptied their minds of everything but its own undeniable presence. All around them and far across the empty floor rose the great columns pillaged from Ephesus and Baalbek, and their muted browns, purples, and rosy pinks glowed coolly in the soft airy light from the semicircular windows a hundred feet above. Everything seemed to float as if the still air, enclosed for more than a millennium, held stone, bronze, marble and mosaic in an effortless suspension, a weightless repose that unified the pomp and splendour of two empires and two religions.

'Walk right across the centre. Towards this side.'

The words were spoken quietly and from a distance and yet it was as if every atom, every speck of dust had vibrated gratingly, resentfully, at the tone of ironic arrogance that lay beneath them. Far away in front of them a shadow moved and a figure appeared silhouetted against the *Mihrab*, the stylized representation of a doorway, set in the wall facing Mecca. The tall spare figure was grotesquely clothed in the revolutionary blouse and beret of Genghiz. Robin, Alp and Dealer moved out from behind the gigantic alabaster urns that flank the Imperial Gate, and began the long walk across the sea of marble.

Genghiz moved towards them a step or two, not to meet them, but to take up a position beneath the centre of the small cupola that covers the apse, with the Virgin and Child glowing in the concave roof behind his head.

'That will do,' he murmured as they approached the shallow step some yards in front of him. 'Now we can talk.'

The echoes died again in the dome two hundred feet above them, and then sounded as Jack and Robin put the case on the floor between them.

Alp grunted and wiped his forehead and the back of his neck with his handkerchief.

'Come on, Genghiz,' he rasped, 'tell us where the girls are. I'll tell my men, and when they're safe we'll let you have the case.'

Genghiz's eyes narrowed and glittered. Quite casually he pulled a gun from the waistband beneath his blotched battle blouse.

'Dealer, Bury, five paces back. Alp, stay where you are.'

He moved forward warily. The safety catch on his pistol clicked solidly. ' "Tell your men", Alp? You have a radio? Put it on the floor two metres in front of me.'

Alp lifted his shoulders and his heavy paw slipped a small transistorized radio out of his breast pocket. Wheezing a little he hoisted himself up the shallow step and gently laid it on the faded rug. He straightened, massaged the small of his back, and smiled. 'Another toy for your armoury,' he said, and renegotiated the step.

Genghiz laughed, took two steps and the radio crunched and snapped beneath his heel.

'We have plenty.' The gun disappeared. He pulled out a cigarette pack, flipped one into his mouth and snapped a flame to it. The blue smoke curled into a sunbeam above their heads—perhaps the first offering of aromatic smoke the Virgin had breathed for five hundred years. The dome did not fall to blot out the blasphemy.

'Now let us get on. No more games, eh, Alp?' He began to speak more briskly. 'We shall take the case. You will wait here for twenty minutes. In seven days, if the contents of the case satisfy us, we shall release Miss Mundham and Miss Liss in a suburb of the city. But every phial must be tested and that will take time even with the facilities we have. After all, it will be high risk work and must be done carefully. If we find that you have not brought what was promised, in the quantity promised, you will find the girls in the Bosporus.'

Robin shook the cold sweat out of his eyes and unclenched his fists; the nails had broken the skin in his palms. At first his voice failed him, then freaked in a near shout before he had it under control.

'You can't expect ... how can we ... we must know they'll be safe, that they'll come back alive, that you won't ask for more.'

Genghiz's white teeth flashed beneath his moustache. 'Really, Mr Bury. There will be little point in keeping two girls to feed when we can hold whole cities to ransom.'

Robin felt almost dizzy with confusion. He glanced at Alp and Jack and met faces blank and expressionless. Genghiz sniggered.

'So Dealer was not quite open with you. Or perhaps not at all. Yes, I think I see it. He wanted a genuine man of the Left, a liberal of undoubted honesty and sincerity to give his charade a veneer of truth. Yes, Dealer, a charade. Do you know when I realized that? The police held you and the Botulin for three days in Istanbul—and then let you travel with it. Either there was no Botulin, or, in spite of appearances, you were working with them. A Kurd died and so did poor Doctor Jones—I think it is Botulin you have there so I am now certain you are working with the Deputy Director. Mr Bury, you have now no one to believe in but me. I at least have told you no lies. Remember this, and persuade your friends to be sensible, or, as I am a truthful man, those girls will float down the Bosporus.'

The bandit snapped a finger. Two men in white coats glided from an alcove. Very quickly the case was lifted and they disappeared the way they had come. Genghiz flicked his cigarette in a high arc over their heads—like a miniature missile with a thread of smoke behind, it tumbled through the air and burst in a tiny shower of sparks behind them. When Bury turned back there was only a haze of vapour where Genghiz had stood and three words hanging in the echoing spaces.

'Remember—twenty minutes.'

Minutes passed and Robin remained on the step in shocked despair. Then his mind began to frame the doubts and questions. Three repeated themselves, as if they were part of a nightmare. What was in the case? Evidently not Pan-mycin. And why was it that Genghiz, Alp, and Dealer shared the knowledge of what was there? And why had Booker been killed?

Alp was standing over the crushed radio, stirring the pieces with his foot.

'I am sorry he did not take it,' he murmured. 'There was a chance he would.'

'A homing device?' Dealer asked.

Alp grunted assent.

'And there wasn't one in the case?' Dealer asked.

'No, they would have found it. You heard Genghiz say they're going to sample every phial. But in the radio it might have been overlooked. Almost certainly it would have been.'

Robin heard the complicity between them, between the Security Police Chief and the International Revolutionary and this proof that Genghiz had spoken the truth added sharpness to an unbearable sense of foreboding.

CHAPTER II

In Alp's office Nur listened in silence to Alp's report of what had happened at Aya Sofia; he lit a cigarette, smoked and thought. At last he spoke, his voice a razor drawn over leather.

'So. He has the girls and the Panmycin.'

Alp said nothing. He even resisted the temptation to shrug fatalistically.

'Is it what he wants?'

'I believe so.'

'I can't think why. If he is dissatisfied, have you anything to offer instead?'

'No. Not immediately. But it is what he wants.'

'Then we must make contact with him again. Through Sami Gunay. Offer him a further ransom—money, freedom and pardon for political prisoners, whatever he wants in exchange for the girls.'

Alp twisted uncomfortably in his chair. He wished he had some raki. He realized he would have to reveal to Nur the true nature of what he still called 'Panmycin' and that when he did there was a risk that he would lose any shred of trust that remained between them. And with the whole operation going so completely wrong he felt he was going to need Nur, both as an ally, and possibly even as a scapegoat. Sweat pricked the back of his paunchy neck as he took what would be an irrevocable step.

His voice was as even as he could make it. 'Genghiz has in his grasp the means to make whatever terms he wants.

Nothing you can offer him can tempt him. That is if his lab tests tell him he has what he thinks he has. And they will.'

Nur waited, suddenly conscious of the strain in Alp's voice and manner. The gravelly voice continued, but now Alp looked at his desk top or at a point where the ceiling touched the wall, not at Nur.

'It is not Panmycin. Not in that particular case. It is Botulin XP3. Genetically engineered bacilli, concentrated, freeze-dried I believe—though I don't pretend to understand the technique. They spread a disease similar to plague but, er, cutting out the middlemen, the fleas and rats. They reactivate and reproduce in water at any temperature between fifteen and thirty-nine degrees centigrade. Genghiz can spread plague in every major city in this country, just whenever he wants.'

Nur turned away, apparently to look out of the window, but it was over a minute before he faced Alp. When he did, his face had changed: a marble-like sheen of moisture had formed on his forehead, his eyes seemed to have receded and they glowed like cold, black star sapphires; his lips were thin and taut, stretched tight over clenched teeth. He had been afflicted, albeit momentarily, with a vision of the aftermath of Armageddon—a city, his city, not Istanbul but Izmir, its palm-lined boulevards quiet and peaceful beneath a burning sun and the pavements strewn with rotting corpses on which vultures and dogs gorged undisturbed. His rational mind had been unable to comprehend what Alp had told him, and, unrestrained, his whole psyche had responded with this terrible illusion which had even filled his nostrils with the stench of putrefaction. He sat heavily in a chair and buried his face in his hands.

Alp looked on helplessly. 'Nur bey ... I'm sorry. Some tea, water, something stronger?'

Nur shook his head violently and straightened. 'That

was foolish,' he muttered. As he went on his voice strengthened. 'Later we may have a chance for you to tell me how this imbecility happened. I am all right, or soon will be. Some tea then. But let us pull ourselves together and try to sort out this mess.'

Alp shouted for tea, and a tea-boy in denims appeared like a shabby djinn. Nur let the sugar suck up the tea almost to his finger before he allowed the crumbling cube to settle to the bottom of the glass. He stirred and sipped.

'Genghiz gave us a week,' he said. 'Have we really that long? Surely he will know that some of this stuff is Botulin XP3 within hours.'

'Yes, but he must suspect that most of the phials are harmless and that we know they are. So he will go on testing. For a week.'

'But every hour his stock of the stuff rises?'

'Yes.'

'And he can use it or threaten to use it as soon as he senses that any sort of pressure is being applied to him.'

'Yes, but he would not be hurried I am sure. He has in his grasp a weapon of unbelievable power. He will want to make the most of it. He will want to prolong its use. He will certainly prefer to use it when he is good and ready and not before.'

'But he will expect some reaction from us.' Nur lit a cigarette. 'He will expect guards on the reservoirs, enquiries at research laboratories, that sort of thing. If none of that happens he may assume the Botulin is harmless—and if he does the girls will die.'

'But that's just it—if we do react, if we do come close to him before he's ready—he has the girls as hostages.'

Nur smoked and drank tea. When he spoke it was with decision. 'Well, they are at risk. The whole country is at risk and we must do the best we can. We must attack him where he expects us to, and vigorously, and hope that we provoke from him a further threat to kill the girls. When the threat comes we respond, but not fully, always we must stay just as near as we dare to forcing him to kill the girls. Only then will he be convinced that we are in earnest and that we have no other plans. Meanwhile less obviously, less conventionally, we must find where he is, where the girls are, and where the Botulin is.'

Alp looked blankly across the darkening room at the white mask on the far side of the desk.

'How?' he grunted.

'Mr Mundham,' said Nur.

Paul Mundham landed at Yeşilkoy Airport off a Lufthansa flight from Frankfurt at noon the next day. He had not slept for thirty-six hours, and for nearly twenty he had been under constant pressure. First he had been thoroughly briefed by Nur; a fast drive to a military airfield had followed, and then the flight to Frankfurt in an American military plane. A few hours later he had boarded the Lufthansa plane back to Istanbul. He took a taxi to the Park Oteli, refused a suite overlooking the Bosporus declaring that all he wanted was a room, coffee and sandwiches, and in less than half an hour he was out again. He kept the same taxi for a swift tour of the city during which he called at the British Consulate, the Police Headquarters, and the Istanbul offices of the Ministry of the Interior; at each stop he made angry demands for the release of his daughter. At the Ministry he was taken behind closed doors ostensibly to see a senior official; in fact he had a shower which was closely supervised by goggled and aproned technicians who then made certain tests with highly sophisticated equipment on his tired and sagging body.

By now the pace was telling. Travel fatigue threatened to overcome him; the bizarre and absurdly dangerous nature of what he was doing threatened to unbalance his sense of reality. Yet determination to find and save his daughter drove him on, and kept at bay the terrible temptation to succumb to exhaustion or escape into emotional collapse.

At five o'clock he returned to the Park Oteli and called a press conference for six. A reporter from the most anti-government paper surviving in Istanbul, and the correspondents of *The Times*, *The Daily Telegraph*, and *The Washington Post* were invited. Next morning all four carried his picture, the story of how his daughter had been in police custody and, so he had finally learnt at the Ministry of the Interior, had been kidnapped under the eyes of the police by urban guerrillas. He said that the police refused to reveal the ransom that had been demanded. In each paper the story ended with the following statement.

'I, Claire Mundham's father, appeal to the Turkish Army of Liberation to make contact with me, to discuss terms for my daughter's release and that of her friend. I am willing to do anything in my power to help my daughter—go anywhere, speak with anyone, pay whatever I can. I offer myself as hostage in place of these girls. The leaders of the Army of Liberation need have no fears —they can arrange their own terms about how and when to make contact: I shall do nothing to jeopardize the safety of my child. But I beg them at any rate to make contact with me.'

In the Turkish paper there was also an editorial claiming that Paul Mundham had no knowledge of or interest in Turkish politics and condemning the police for incompetence, vacillation, lack of respect for family ties, and various other vices.

Throughout the day the world press arrived and infested the Park. At five o'clock British T.V. crews arrived from Crete where they had been filming a glossy spy serial. But Paul was unaware of any of this: mildly sedated and with a police guard outside his door he managed to get some sort of rest.

At half past five the phone rang in Alp's office. He switched on the speaker and Nur leaned forward to listen.

'Alp bey?'

'Speaking.'

'Genghiz here. Alp bey, you are playing a dangerous game. When I heard Mr Mundham had visited you I wondered what you were up to, and I nearly slit the girls' throats—to be on the safe side. Then we got the newspaper story last night just before they put the paper to bed and I thought this Alp Vural is a very clever man—he thinks he can kill me with laughter. But now I have slept on it and talked with my general staff and here is what we have to say.'

'Go on.' Alp's fingers whitened over the receiver and with his free hand he patted at the back of his neck with a handkerchief. Nur stubbed at the blotter with his pen.

'Just possibly,' the voice resumed with the smoothness of oil on graphite stone, 'Mr Mundham's story is true. That is immaterial. Whether it is or not you must now hope we will pick him up, and allow you to fix our whereabouts through him. Well, we will see him, we will take him to his daughter, but it must be done our way. The world press is giving us very good coverage and it will put us even more in the public eye if we manage to kidnap Mr Mundham too, and, like his daughter, from police protection. Just at this time we want all the publicity we can get. We would like to have American, Russian, and even Japanese television here for our next step. You see Alp, those phials do contain Botulin XP3 or at least the first twenty do, and I'm disposed to take your word about the rest. In any case if a random sample of fifty turn out right we shall go ahead. And when we threaten to pollute the reservoirs of every major city with Plague we want the eyes of the world here, just in case your government feels it can keep the true nature of the threat from the Turkish people. And we should also like to be sure that the people know just how this stuff came to be in our country in the first place. In short the public outcry as the first few unfortunates swell up and die must be such that you will be forced to accept our terms. So for the sake of the publicity, we will take Mundham, but under our conditions, of course.'

'Of course.'

'Listen carefully then...'

At nine o'clock there was a knock on Paul's door. Wearily he came out of a daydream about the dahlias just about bursting into first bloom in his Heathleigh garden, hauled himself to his feet and slipped on his jacket. He opened the door. A young policeman in plain clothes flashed his identification which Paul had been taught to recognize and came in. Paul thought he knew him as the officer who had driven his daughter from Siirt to Istanbul. Paul rather liked the look of him—more like the brighter sort of lad one got straight from Grammar School applying for jobs which needed a bit of initiative and drive if you were going to make a go of them.

'It's working Mr Mundham,' he said. 'I am to take you to Alp bey's office, but on the way you will be kidnapped. This is how Genghiz has asked for it to be arranged.'

'Oh, right. Very good, very good.' Paul felt a painful constriction in his barrel chest and a sudden difficulty in breathing. He dug his nails into his palms and the room stopped swinging and the pain melted. He straightened his jacket, his R.A.F. tie, and smoothed the tufts of hair behind his ears.

'Very good then. Just as you say.'

Gökalp took him to a service lift, and then out through the kitchens to the delivery bays at the back of the hotel.

A black Mercedes with police registration plates was waiting, and a policeman in black uniform stood over it, his fingers stuck in his white gun belt.

Gökalp held open the rear door for Paul and took the driver's seat. The policeman saluted and stood aside. Gökalp breathed deeply and reached for the ignition.

'Er, could you tell me what's going to happen before we start? I mean if we've, um, time.'

Gökalp looked at his watch and leant back.

'We drive down on to Necati Bey Caddesi, the road that leads along the Bosphorus to the Galata Quay where the liners dock. Before we get there we shall be stopped at a corner where the road goes right to the water's edge. You will be taken out and put into a power boat.'

'It sounds simple enough.' Paul tried to sound confident. Gökalp shrugged.

'It is arranged that I should resist, and that they shall ... silence me. I am not expected to be hurt much.'

He wiped his palms on the knees of his trousers and reached again for the ignition. The car purred, slid up a steep ramp and then they began to drop through the back streets towards the water.

'It must be horrid knowing for sure that you must be injured.' Paul felt the young man's fear with biting keenness. He had an urge to tell him to stop or turn back and then found it strange that such a thought had even entered his head—odd that his feeling for Gökalp who was nothing to him had momentarily driven out his longing for Claire's safety.

The road levelled. To the left the Dolmabahce Palace, the last rococo excess of a dying dynasty, floated ghostlike above the black, swift water. They turned right down a wide boulevard that had been torn through the ancient wooden houses that had once lined the caesura between Europe and Asia—a few broken shells still waited for the bulldozers, black skeletons rising from mounds of dusty rubble. A line of drab warehouses came between them and the water, the road angled and narrowed round them, and there in front was a parked ambulance, and three men in white overalls, caught in the headlights. The men had guns.

'Get down Mr Mundham, right down.' Gökalp's voice was raised, peremptory but controlled, like an angry schoolmaster's. The big car surged forward, accelerating fast, Paul felt the rear seat lurch into his back, and he rolled with it into an awkward crouch on the floor as noise burst with appalling suddenness on his eardrums. A hail of bullets smashed into tyres, grille and windscreen, tearing rubber, crumpling metal, exploding glass. With its support systems smashed, spilling oil, water and petrol on to the tarmac, the car slid, jolted and, with a scream of tortured metal, ground to a standstill.

Through numbed ears Mundham barely sensed the sounds of running feet, a distant shout and the kick and slam of the driver's door. He lifted his head and saw Gökalp in the middle of the road, in the act of levelling a police issue thirty-eight. Paul's voice rasped a horrified shout, one of the white-coated men dropped to a knee and from barely ten yards pumped shells at the young policeman. As if caught by a whirlwind the body spun, was lifted and dropped—a shapeless heap of rags and torn flesh pumping blood into the oily grit beneath him.

The door behind Paul was wrenched open, hands clamped on his shoulders and dragged him backwards; light and pain exploded at the back of his head as it caught the lintel; he was hauled to his feet and sent sprawling, crawling, stumbling and at last running towards the parapet beyond the ambulance. More hands pulling and tearing bundled him over, smacking him on to the hardwood floor of a powered inflatable. His chest hurt, his eyes swam, pain, shock and horror stormed his brain centres yet a corner of his consciousness registered a strange pleasure at recognizing the craft he was in: it was like the one he had at home and used for pottering about in the Thames estuary. Harsh shouts echoed in his ear, the painter smacked on the floor beside him and the powerful outboard motor roared into life.

As the flat-bottomed speedboat flung itself in a wide curve out into the blackness Alp Vural reached the parapet, panting from the hundred metres sprint that had brought him from the cover of the warehouses. The tired gross man peered out into the gloom, his eyes then his ears straining after the phosphorescent wake and the pounding engine, until sight and sound were swallowed in the darkness.

At last he turned and walked slowly back to Gökalp's body.

CHAPTER III

During their second confinement together Claire found
Donna an even more trying cell-mate than she had the
first time. Then there had been the awkwardness of
establishing a mutually satisfactory level of intimacy,
avoiding unpleasant coldness on one side and a distasteful
closeness on the other. No such problem arose this time—
Donna remained withdrawn, obsessed with her own private
world of horror. Her behaviour varied—sometimes she
would sit on the floor with her knees under her chin, making patterns in the dust with a languid finger, or she would
pace around their oddly shaped cell, backwards and for-
wards like a caged cat. The simile was apt: they had been
put in a semicircular gazebo which had been built out of
wood and glass on to the end of a small house overlooking
the Marmora. The curved wall was glazed down to waist
height with a window seat below, and secured on the
outside with iron bars. The whole structure gave an exposed, cage-like feeling to their situation.

At other times Donna drifted into a sort of Ophelia
state. She would move about the small area in swinging
little dancing steps that were ghosts of the movements she
had made with Booker at the Red Pasha Disco, humming
snatches of tunes, clicking her fingers, pausing to adjust
her curls or her neckline when her reflection in one of
the panes caught her eye.

But the times Claire feared her most, when she seemed
completely beyond reach, were at dusk on all three times

night had fallen. Then, when there was still enough light to see your hand in front of you, but the darkness had thickened to the point where the guards were an indistinct mass that could have been a bush or a bear, then Donna would sit on the floor with her back to the windowseat, delve deep into her bag and produce the Gestapo knife she had bought in the Bazaar. Mostly she just looked at it, but occasionally she made little jabbing movements so that the narrow flanged blade flashed in reflected light from the windows of the house.

Claire had suggested that the knife might be useful in an escape attempt. She had not meant this seriously —her aim had been to break into the mind of the American girl, a mind which seemed a worse prison than their cell.

'I shall use this once,' Donna had said and her eyes had widened and glittered like a cat's. 'Just once, on the man who killed Booker.' She slipped the knife in its sheath and buried it deep in her duffle bag. Then she edged closer to Claire, put her hand on the English girl's knee. 'Which is it Claire? Who killed my Booker? Was it Jack? A Kurd? That fat policeman, or the nice-looking serious one? Or Robin?' She sensed a shudder which had surprised Claire herself. 'You wouldn't want it to be Robin, would you chicken?'

Claire sniffed.

'Poor Claire. No more of Booker's pills. All gone.'

The third night wore on. At eleven o'clock a quiet conversation outside signalled the two-hourly change of guard and Claire began at last to feel her eyelids growing irresistibly heavy. Distantly the sound of a power boat throbbed across the sea. It came nearer, was loud, and then died. There was a shout, and running footsteps from the house. A light from the sea swung across the glass roof of the gazebo. Claire sat up on the straw palliasse that was their only bedding and then pulled herself to her feet.

Outside there was more light than usual spilling from the house to her right and torches glimmered and weaved down by the water's edge where there were two boat houses. The guard outside stiffened as he sensed she was watching behind him, but he made no move. Straw rustled and Donna breathed at her shoulder.

'What is it?'

'I don't know. A boat came. Someone's arrived.'

The torches swung towards them as a group left the boat houses and crossed the lawns. Four men stepped into the pool of light—one led the way, two supported the fourth between them.

'Oh, God!' cried Claire, 'it's Daddy! They've got Daddy.'

Perhaps her cry was loud enough to be heard, perhaps Paul Mundham sensed that she was watching him. He shrugged off the men and stood for a moment alone. In spite of his rumpled clothes, his terribly drawn face that had aged five years in as many days, he managed to look solid, erect, firm. The tears that ran down Claire's cheeks, real tears not hay-fever, sprang from overwhelming relief.

The City was at risk. One and a half million souls crammed into a few square miles—millionaires and beggars, diamond smugglers and students, business men, clerks, dustmen and dockers, and their wives and children—all faced a worse crisis than that of 1918 when the allied fleets steamed up the Bosporus. In the sixth century their ancestors had been amongst the first in the West to be decimated by Plague—now the ancient scourge threatened again.

In a large rectangular room in the heart of the Belediye Nur and Alp had the city's resources at their disposal. All branches of the police were on emergency standby and the army was out. A hastily formed unit of epidemi-ologists were in permanent conference with the engineers who controlled the water supplies and sewerage, and the hospitals had been emptied of all but the most dangerously ill and then isolated. The room was crowded—more crowded than either Alp or Nur would have liked. Senators who represented the city had flown back from Ankara, there was a handful of generals, and perhaps worst of all, Bitterne himself had reappeared. No one had suggested that Alp should cease to be in charge of the operation. The possibility and consequence of failure were far too obvious.

One wall of the room was covered entirely with an illuminated map of enormous scale—half a metre to the kilometre. Clerks often making use of ladders on wheels that glided along the floor beneath it, hatched and cross-hatched areas in red, green, and finally black to the instruc-tions of a further group of men stationed behind a long bank of telephones. Already about a fifth of the map had been shaded out at least once, and about a tenth of it with all three colours, but now, at about the time on the second night after his capture that Paul was reunited with his daughter, progress was slower as the telephone calls came in with less and less frequency.

Behind the telephone bank Alp and Nur stood, smoking, drinking tea, occasionally exchanging restrained comments beneath the subdued babble and movement of over a hundred people.

An aide glided up to them and coughed quietly.

'Admiral Revere has arrived, bey effendi, and would like to speak to you. The C-in-C of NATO forces, East Mediterranean.'

Nur turned to see a stout bespectacled American of about sixty in battledress and cap with gold-encrusted peak. The admiral looked paunchy and pink, but his eyes were shrewd and he was painstakingly courteous.

'How's it going?' he asked in a soft New England accent, after quiet introductions had been made.

Alp gestured at the map.

'The red hatching signifies areas where they are most likely to be, green the ones that have been gone over carefully, black the areas that have been checked out completely either by house to house search, or by geiger counters where there was a real possibility of their presence in the first place.'

'How long have you been at it?'

'Twenty-four hours. If we are unlucky it could be another four days. If they have given Mr Mundham a shower it could be never. Or if they have taken him more than twenty kilometres away.'

'What range do the geigers have?'

'There are two sorts. We have five that were made especially for the radioactive soap Mr Mundham was washed in—they pinpoint sources of just that radiation and no other up to three hundred metres. We have another ten borrowed from NATO and adapted, but they have a range of only one hundred metres and they pick up other sources of radiation as well.'

'Still, it all helps.'

Nur intervened.

'I'm not sure. A hundred metres is very close. The guerrillas could easily spot the detector vans and be on the alert even if they don't realize what they are for. And when they do pick up radiation we have to check it out very carefully, or waste time getting the nearest specialist detector over.' Nur smiled wryly. 'They have already uncovered a shipment of Swiss watches with luminous dials and a small cache of phosphorus bombs.'

'Perhaps I can pull strings, cut red tape, and get you some more.'

'Thanks, but I doubt if even you can. Of the five good ones two were flown out from Brussels, one from London, and one from Bonn. The fifth is yours anyway and is mounted on a cutter that's checking out the east side of the Bosporus right now.'

'I meant from Stateside. Jumbos could have another ten or twenty here within twenty-four hours.'

Nur shrugged. Twenty-four hours was the span he felt they had before Genghiz would begin moving the Botulin XP3 into tactical positions. When that happened the whole operation would take on a quite different shape.

'Anyway I'll see what I can do.' Admiral Revere padded away to the dimmer recesses of the hall to find his Flag Officer and make the necessary signals.

Nearby Her Britannic Majesty's Chargé d'Affaires approached Bitterne whom he had met before.

'Forsdike of the F.O.,' he said, offering a hand. 'Bitterne, isn't it?' He knew it was—Bitterne's dome with its ginger nimbus was unforgettable.

Bitterne admitted the identification reluctantly.

'I say, this radioactive soap, won't it damage this Mundham chap?'

'Good question. As far as we know no one's had it on before for so long and in that concentration. He won't suffer burns, but he might be sterilized, and there might be long term effects—bone cancer, leukaemia, that sort of thing.'

Forsdike found Bitterne irritatingly cool about it.

'I suppose he knew the risks?'

'I guess so.'

'Jolly brave chap. Good war record, I gather.'

Bitterne moved away. He was feeling rather miserable. Chester Harrisburg, Vice President of the General Drug Company, had reacted swiftly and badly to the news of Booker Jones's death. Apparently the doctor had been a very promising employee, likely to do well in the firm besides being a showcase item because of his ethnic origin ... and so on. The likely upshot of it all was that it now seemed that there would be no place for Bitterne on the payroll, and he had not yet found the courage to break this news to his wife. It had been her naggingly repeated dissatisfaction with his present job that had led him to consider complicating the operation with the addition of Booker Jones and real Panmycin: the G.D.C., which had, for some time, been putting pressure on the Agency to find some way of testing the drug in the field, had promised to pay well—but only for results.

The night wore on. Long before dawn the older captains and ministers had departed yawning, after muttering earnest instructions that they should be called if the situation changed radically. Meanwhile the grey, unmarked vans idled up and down the deserted alleys and thoroughfares of the City and out at sea the cutter turned the corner of the Bosporus and headed east along the north coast of the Marmora, its radar-like antenna searching for the radioactive skin of the Englishman.

Shortly before dawn one more flurry of activity ruffled the dimmed and hushed atmosphere of the Operations Room. At the back of the hall voices were raised—argumentative, issuing firm negatives, and then angry. Bitterne, who had been standing in front of the map, identified one of the voices and spotted the unkempt, tinted yellow hair amongst the helmets and peaked caps of guards and police. Jack Dealer had talked himself in.

'Bitterne, is that you? Tell these gooks the kind of clearance I have, will you?' Dealer was waving two bits of paper. Bitterne pushed his way through.

'You've got them, then.'

'Of course I have. Now get me in and take me to Colonel Nur or whoever's running this end now. And get these gooks off of me—they stink of garlic—before I lay one out.'

'O.K., Jack, O.K. You can't blame them. Let's see your authorization.'

'Here you are. One from the Turkish Minister and one cabled from the Pentagon.'

'O.K., they're O.K.' Since he was morally certain that Dealer had killed Doctor Jones, Bitterne was not as sympathetic to his colleague as he might have been. 'Now just wait here while I see Colonel Nur Arslan and Deputy Director Alp Vural. They're not going to like this one bit: all right Jack—I know they're going to have to live with it. But if they're going to work with you you'll want them feeling fairly flexible about it, so just let me have a quiet word with them first. Now you just sit here, get yourself a coffee—there's a machine, have you got twenty-five kurush? Right. I'll be right back.'

Bitterne padded back up the hall and cleared his throat at Alp's shoulder.

'Er, Jack Dealer's got his clearance.'

It sank in slowly—their eyes were fixed on the black line edging slowly along the Marmora coast as the cutter radioed negatives. But they looked angry when they turned.

'Let me see.' Alp took the documents in his podgy hairy hand and studied them. 'He's got everything but the President's signature.' He meant the one in Ankara.

Bitterne spoke quickly and apologetically. 'I know how you feel about him, and I can see your point of view, but this is still a joint operation, and it can still achieve what it set out to do, and we are rightly insisting on having an operative in at the kill. Don't try and block this. We could take all our hardware out, you know—the spotter plane, the choppers, the detectors. You might as well let him along for the ride.'

Nur drew breath. 'Why Dealer? Why not you or one of the others?'

'Hell, you know I can't do that. I'm control, he's the operative. There's a proper form about these things.'

Nur glanced at his watch. The first gleam of sunlight

would be touching gold candle flames to the crescents on the minarets and out at Yeşilköy airport the spotter plane would be warming its engines for another day circling the sky high above the City. He suppressed emotion, calculated cold risk against cold risk.

'Inshallah. So be it.' He turned back to the map. His voice choked as if at something totally abhorrent. 'I hate killers.'

Paul Mundham sat as upright as he could on the window seat. That way there was only a single pane of glass and a hundred yards of air between him and the sea. In front of him, through cedars and cypresses, the bosky hills of Asia darkened into sharper outline as the sun rose behind them. Distantly the muezzin called and the traffic began to rumble along the main road to Ankara. Perhaps from that side too the detector would come.

On his lap was Claire's hand. He clasped it, for his hands had not been soaped, and let her head rest on his jacketed shoulder. He was cold and he looked forward to the warmth of the sun. Donna lay stretched out in front of him, her head pillowed on the duffle bag which her arms circled possessively. He had been there for little more than half an hour. Since his arrival he had been questioned again, this time by Genghiz, and suffered his second body search in twenty-four hours. But they had not washed him, nor had he asked for a bath.

He had told Claire and Donna all he knew. The original plot had been simple in principle but devious and complex in execution. The plan had been to discredit the far left movement, to alienate what popular support it had, by arranging for its leaders to be caught in possession of Botulin XP3. He explained what Botulin XP3 was. He also explained how Claire and Donna had been made to believe that it had come from Russia in the hope that they would testify to that in a public enquiry or trial.

'But Booker was shot,' Claire protested.

Donna stirred. 'No chick. I realized that later when I saw the wound. He wouldn't let me see it until it was almost healed. It was a knife wound. I know the difference. Jack Dealer fired all those shots. In the air.'

Claire remembered, as if in a dream, the smell of cordite that had clung to Dealer on the Thracian hillside.

'Why did Booker put up with that?'

'He did it to himself, honey.' The first shaft of sunlight gleamed in Donna's hair. 'You know he was employed by the General Drug Company. Two of those cases were Panmycin. The G.D.C. wanted them tested; they were in a hurry; a Swiss company had nearly negotiated a licence with the Russians and the G.D.C. had to move quickly to get their own version on the market. But if anything went wrong the G.D.C. wanted the world to think it was Russian Panmycin that was twisted. It was a hell of a thing for Booker to do, but they had promised him a clinic in Harlem and another in the south near where he was born. And all along it was a cover for this Botulin shit. Booker knew nothing about that although I expect G.D.C makes it too.'

'But why was Booker killed? He didn't treat those three Kurds with Botulin.'

'No dear,' said Paul. 'Two of those cases did have Panmycin in. Dealer would have made sure that those were the ones he used.'

Donna seemed to choke or sob—it was difficult to say which. Then she recovered and the gold bangles in her ears gleamed.

'No,' she said, 'that's not right. The children got Panmycin, but after we had gone the boy with the leg got Botulin.'

'But how?'

'Don't you remember at Ipsala, the customs officer. He

took samples from each case, from each tray. At least one of the plague phials, perhaps a tray of them, must have been put back in the wrong case.'

Paul was distracted by a trim cutter that was slowly chugging across the bay in front of them, barely a hundred metres from the shore. It disappeared behind the boat houses.

Donna raced on. 'So Barzani's nephew died. And Booker worked all night to find out why. He discovered plague and Dealer killed him.' She caught her breath again and the sun lit her face. 'I know who to kill.'

Paul gazed at her with eyes clouded with terrible fatigue, but his ears registered that the cutter circled round and was coming back from the east.

'Just as you ... say, dear.' His voice faded and his head nodded forward.

CHAPTER IV

'It's it, they've found him.' A young man with spectacles was on his feet in the middle of the bank of telephones. The hall froze for a second and then there was a concerted movement to the front. But Alp was there first.

He took the receiver and his free hand swung up in a florid gesture of command.

'*Shushumbay!* Be quiet.' His voice boomed out like the note of a sixty-four foot organ pipe.

In the total silence they could hear the murmur of the telephone, then Alp bent his thick trunk across the console and gesticulated at the petrified marker at the far right of the map.

'It's the cutter.' His voice had returned to its habitual croak, but lost none of its urgency. 'Moda Bay, almost exactly half way between Moda and Fenerbahce, just where the Ankara highway is nearest to the sea. They say it's a wooden villa, with a built-on gazebo at the east end. Trees behind. Two boathouses on the water's edge. To the west modern villas, three of them, an apartment block, eight storeys. To the east wasteland and then a "plage" with cafés and pleasure boats.'

The marker running his finger over the map, stopped, retracked.

'This is it, this must be it.'

Nur ran round the console and joined him. He took the felt tip pen and drew a black arrow up from the sea so the point just touched the coastline beneath the tiny box that indicated the villa's grounds.

They all stood back and looked at the map. The Bosporus, thirty kilometres long, bisected it from north to south in a stretched out 'S'. At its southern end it widened into the Marmora Sea and on these two southern corners stand the two halves of Istanbul. On the Asian, eastern side the line of the coast runs north-west to south-east in a succession of shallow bays and headlands and the arrow stood in the first of those that truly belong to the Marmora and not the Bosporus. It is a rather derelict, run-down area, not yet developed like the commercial centre of Moda where the Red Pasha Disco was, not like the smart suburb of Fenerbahce that stands on its eastern headland.

Entirely revitalized Nur and Alp began to put the next phase into operation.

'The cutter must return north to Kadikoy. I want the nearest detector van passing that villa in two hours precisely, the cutter to return then as well to give us an exact fix on where Mundham is. Keep lines open to the cutter and the van, cut the other vans' lines and open new ones as you have been instructed.'

One of these was to the spotter plane, and Nur was soon in touch with the Turkish interpreter who shared the cockpit with the American flier. He gave an exact map reference and asked for conditions; atmospherics crackled in his ear and then cleared.

'A ceiling of cirro-stratus at eight thousand metres, banks of low cloud over the hills to the east which are weakening the sun, but should clear soon. Some patches of sea mist in the area but they're not likely to interfere and they'll go soon. He says we'll get good pictures from seven thousand metres but they'll improve as the sun gets up.'

Nur turned to an American adviser. 'Is seven thousand metres all right?'

'It's fine. He can circle there all day and they'll never notice him. And because it's near the airport and civil flights are coming down or going up he's clear of the air lanes. But one fly-past from a chopper will get you horizontal pictures, and they'll be worth much more.'

'We can risk one helicopter buzz—the guerrillas must be expecting some activity of that sort all over the city. Get me the heliport.'

But here there was a setback.

'No choppers today, bey effendi.'

'Why ever not?'

'Control at the heliport says they'll be grounded over the Bosporus for at least two days. It's the storks.'

Nur looked round helplessly. An Istanbul policeman came to the rescue.

'Early October—the migrating storks, they come from all over Europe on their way to the south. They hate crossing the water and so they gather here twice a year, thousands, perhaps hundreds of thousands, and for two days they'll fill the air above the city. It's an extraordinary sight before they get themselves across and on their way again.'

'Never mind,' said Alp, 'we'll have pictures from the cutter in a few hours.'

Outside the sun climbed and bright daylight flooded the city, a city unaware of the danger it faced, yet excited as it always is when the storks come; everywhere people stopped and pointed, not only tourists stopped—for the sight never fails to catch the imagination of the regular Istanbulis. From the north and west the 'V'-shaped formations of huge birds come winging in over domes and palaces, check at the water, and then flock in spirals in the thermals above the European side where they soar and sink in ever increasing thousands before dusk comes. Then the supporting air cools and they have to gather courage and from the tops of failing thermals launch themselves across to the other side. But the windowless Operations Centre knew none of this. Information poured in, reports, hypotheses, confirmations, and at last photographs. Decisions had to be made about the final phase.

Differences of interest clashed. Alp and the City chiefs wanted a ring of steel, including gun-boats, a *cordon sanitaire*, round the villa. The guerrillas would be given an ultimatum and if this was not accepted the place would be razed with rockets and mortars. Their reasoning was that only in this way could they be absolutely sure that not one phial of Botulin XP3 could get out, and they declared that that should be everybody's first objective.

Nur was not convinced and he had much difficulty in persuading them that his concern was not merely for the lives of the three hostages, though they would certainly be lost if such strategy was used.

'There are two other factors,' Nur pointed out patiently. 'One—it is most unlikely that the Botulin is in the villa—Genghiz is hardly likely to keep both his weapons in the same place; two—we are not even sure that Genghiz himself is there. But put yourself in his place. Until he has the Botulin ready to be fed into the water supply it is no use to him, it doesn't guarantee his safety. But the hostages do give him some protection. My guess is he will stay with the hostages until his supporters say they can threaten the whole city. Only then will he leave the villa. We must rescue the hostages and capture or kill Genghiz before that happens.'

He found unexpected and not too welcome support from Dealer and Bitterne. They still hoped to catch, preferably in the lens of a good camera, and in front of neutral witnesses, Genghiz with his hands on the case of Botulin XP3, and this they reckoned they might still achieve with Nur's plan. Alp, under pressure from his Director who had worked with the Americans from the beginning, began to waver.

At eleven o'clock the fix from the cutter and the detector van was confirmed by the first photographs and it was certain that Mundham and the girls were in the gazebo. It was later discovered that the villa had no cellar or attic and the gazebo with its bars was an obvious cell. With this news it did seem possible that a selective attack on a smaller scale might succeed.

Lunch they took standing up—the sort of meal anyone can buy from kiosks in a Turkish city: toasted cheese sandwiches, rolls with thick slices of dill-flavoured pickled cucumber, discs of smoked mutton heavily flavoured with garlic and coated with paprika. They drank glasses of tea or tumblers of freshly crushed pomegranate, apple, peach, or pear juice, and the thick smoke of Bafra tobacco began to layer and swirl in the high ceiling above their heads in spite of the air-conditioning. And at last they heard that Genghiz was in the villa.

The attack was planned for one hour before sunset and would be launched from the west, out of the sun, and from the north—the two approaches which would allow the detachment of marines led by NCOs who were Korean veterans to get within a hundred metres of the villa with almost no possibility of their being detected. Further troops would surround the villa at a distance to cut off a guerrilla break out.

The troops would be armed with automatic NATO rifles, four rocket launchers, and grenades—CS gas, smoke and non-fragmentary offensive. The attack was to be opened with twenty seconds intensive bombardment, directed at all the windows and was to be followed by an immediate assault on foot. They calculated that the guerrillas would have no chance to organize a first stage resistance—with luck the first marines would be in the house, or what was left of it, without any shots being fired at them. The Colonel of marines reckoned that it would all be over in less than ninety seconds and that this gave a very reasonable chance of rescuing the hostages before they were murdered.

Nur Arslan disagreed.

They now had well-defined blow-ups of the gazebo—in one of them they could clearly see Paul Mundham's back —and in all of them two or three guards in para-military uniform patrolled within ten yards of the barred glass-house. Moreover, one shot from the east showed a window above the gazebo and the silhouette of another guard framed in it. An expert in counter-insurgency studied these figures under a magnifying glass and pronounced that they were probably carrying grenades in the top pockets of their battledresses. There was no one there who did not recall that hostages had once been killed by grenades in a house on the Black Sea coast.

'That gazebo,' said Nur, 'has a glass roof. It would take very considerably less than ninety seconds to drop a grenade in from above, or lob one in from outside.'

'Isn't there a chance that the guards will just run as soon as the villa is attacked?' asked Bitterne.

'No chance at all,' the counter-insurgency expert murmured. 'It is an absolute article of faith with these men that as soon as they are threatened, hostages are killed. Otherwise the policy of taking hostages loses all credibility.'

'I wouldn't risk a rocket on that window,' said the Colonel of marines, 'but at three hundred metres my best shots could blot it out with automatic fire. But as long as the outside guards are between my men and the gazebo I can't pick them off without shooting up the gazebo too. And the ground between us and them is broken, and a wounded man could find enough cover to be safe for a minute or so and a wounded man can lob a grenade.'

Alp rasped. 'I'm afraid Nur's asking for the moon. They'll just have to take their chance.'

Nur thought of Paul Mundham, of Claire, of Donna— their bodies torn, disfigured, blasted, burnt. He thought of how long a wrecked, bombed body can bleed in agony before the release of death or morphine arrives.

'I think we must do better than that.' He spoke quietly. 'Let's have Robin Bury in.'

CHAPTER V

Two hours before sunset Robin took the longer of the two ferry crossings from Europe to Asia, the one that leaves in front of Sinan's New Mosque at the mouth of the Golden Horn, passes round Seraglio Point, threads its way through tankers and cargo boats lying at anchor in the roads, runs parallel to the long sea wall in front of Haydarpasha Station, and drops you at Kadikoy landing stage. It must be the most spectacular ferry trip in the world (though better from east to west), and most especially so in the very late afternoon, and in October when the storks are still soaring and sailing above the old city. The sun was still high enough and south enough to light the domes and minarets of the three great mosques, to set fire to the ochre stone of the enormous battlements, and yet low enough to throw purple shadows where it no longer shone.

Bury felt little or nothing at this splendour, though he would have liked to, for he was sure he was on his way to die. Yet he did not feel fear, just blankness, emptiness, drained. It was as if the thinking, sentient part of his mind had been switched off, and he had become an automaton, a robot, that could receive impressions, store them, even act upon them, but consider them not at all. A mild interest was the most emotion he could muster and perhaps a faint feeling of awe at the length and height of the Russian tanker along whose lee they passed, a faint temptation to answer the wave of a seaman who flourished a mop high above over the bow of the giant ship. He read the

Cyrillic script, *Potemkin Odessa* and noticed the racing of the water along the plimsoll line. There must be a strong current—of course, here the Black Sea empties into the Marmora—and his gaze wandered out over the sea, choppy and dark, the colour of darkest slate. A caïque, sails furled, chugged wearily up against the flow of water, pushing itself north to the Golden Horn with a cargo of melons.

Haydarpasha with its quays, derricks and railway terminal was now on the port bow, soon they would be there. Near the ferry station he would find a rank of shared taxis, 'dolmushler', with their destinations printed on their windscreens. He would find one labelled 'Fenerbahce', a red Chevrolet, very old. He was to pay no attention to the other passengers and without being told the driver would drop him at the villa. Then ... Robin pushed aside the thought of 'then'.

It was odd he thought, ironic if you like, he had spent most of his adult life fighting for what he had once called 'liberal' causes. As a teenager he had marched to Aldermaston and, in later years, back again. Even before that his feet had been trodden on by a police horse in Whitehall at the time of Suez. And then it had got more earnest, there had been real freedoms, at home, to fight for: London School of Economics in the middle sixties; the coming of the underground; the Maoist dialectic not only condoning violence, but urging it. He had gone along with that, he had studied the texts, the evidence, Fanon and Marcuse, applied the disciplines of his own subject and lectured on them from the standpoint of the Levi-Straussian social anthropologist. Finally he had offered himself in action, to assist the Turkish Army of Liberation—but with Panmycin, the cure-all, not plague. And here he was now on his way, he supposed, to die, an accessory to the forces of reaction, assisting in the destruction of the Movement in Turkey.

Why? Not really because of the Botulin XP3—that had,

after all, been provided by the Americans and their vomit was their responsibility. But to give a better chance of life to a rather ordinary, elderly business man and his daughter, and the American girl. It was the fallacy, he told himself, of all white, bourgeois radicals—a man, and two girls whom he knew against the freedoms of millions. The man and especially one of the girls. When Colonel Nur had told him that he might save Claire from being blown to bits, he had known that he would have to go.

The ferry nudged the landing stage and clutching the tasselled bag with its two dull, steel, sinister canisters in it, he let himself be carried forward in the tide of early commuters, hurrying home to their Asian villas and apartments from the grey office blocks of Europe.

He walked across a road of large flat cobbles, stepped over a half-eaten water-melon and thought for a moment that the red, torn flesh was covered with black flies—but they were seeds—and, still jostled by the commuters, found the rank of dolmushler. The first two were going to Suadiye, the third to Fenerbahce. It was red, a Chevrolet, very old—the wings and high fins crumpled, the chrome peeling. A pang of anxiety—it was full. Five men with attaché cases packed on the back bench, two in the front with the driver. But the nearest passenger threw open the door and twelve inches of space appeared on the seat beside him. Robin folded himself in and managed to shut the door against his right leg.

The driver pressed the big chrome button, the hood shuddered and the beads, ribbons and tiny Koran on the rear-view mirror began to sway. The Chevrolet slid out into the traffic.

Not a word was said. Robin could not see who was behind him, but he felt he was known, was being watched. He wondered if they had all been on the ferry with him. They found the main Ankara freeway and the surroundings became suburban. Houses and apartments were more widely spaced and there were trees. Robin remembered that he had already been down this road twice—out with Claire, and back with Dealer. He felt sick when he thought of Dealer—really ready to vomit. He swallowed and wiped his palms on his trousers.

The dolmush slowed down and pulled into the kerb. Beyond the driver he could see pines and cypresses, rather stunted and drab, two flaky gate-posts and he recognized them from the photographs which he had studied three hours before. An arm reached from behind, squeezed past his shoulder, and released the catch on the door. A voice murmured in his ear.

'Allah usmaladek—go with God.'

Robin looked at his watch. Two minutes early. He wanted to pee, could feel moisture drying and salt prickling all over his body. His eyes smarted and he wondered if this was how Claire felt when her hay-fever hit her. Urgently he made himself think, almost talked to himself. All people, he thought, fulfilled themselves in the end. Not in any grand way, but simply because they are what they are—their actions mirror their choices, and no two people are the same and no science or pseudo science can catch their elusive but basic individuality. Does Literature? Claire would say so. Consider them. If Paul Mundham is anything, he is a father and now he is most a father. Donna a Leftie, drawn as if by a whirlpool from the outer edges of politics to violence—somewhere or sometime she would have forced or created just such a crisis for herself. Booker Jones corrupted by his intelligence, and by the computerized corporation he had worked for....

An oil tanker thundered by and Robin started, looked at his watch—he was now fifteen seconds late. For a further two seconds he was frozen, glued to the ground by many

more Gs than ever an astronaut felt at maximum accelera-
tion, held by the pull of his desire to live—that psychic
gravity that anchors us to earth, to life, to survival—the
gravity which man alone, by will, can push through. Robin
moved.

Desperately he clung to his train of thought as trees,
browned grasses, untidy gravel flowed slowly by. Dealer—
the 'agent provocateur', determined to see the end of his
work, the Judas not content with silver, along to see the
Crucifixion, and now somewhere over there to the left
with Nur bey. Nur bey—the perfect policeman? Robin
smiled wryly—even fuzz are fab. Nur spending his life
sorting out the blundering stupidities of people, so the
least possible pain was suffered by people. This must be
the first bend in the drive. A building through the trees,
glass—what did they call it? Gazebo. They mustn't stop
him here, too soon, he must get nearer. He quickened
his stride. And Claire—what was she, to be found at such
risk? The eternal princess of archetypal myths, Andro-
mache chained to the rock, menaced by the sea monster,
the king her father helpless, the whole population waiting
for her deliverance, for their deliverance. I'm being fanci-
ful now, thought Robin. A touch ridiculous, for that
would make Genghiz the dragon that the reactionary
press saw him as, and it would make me Perseus, Saint
George....

'Dur! Kim O?'

(Nur Arslan, two hundred yards to his left, sucked in
his cheeks and raised a flare pistol in one hand, and held
his binoculars steady with the other. Two guards between
him and the gazebo, one had seen Bury and challenged
him.)

Robin, almost in the end of the drive, almost at the
point where it spread itself into a forecourt, halted, and,
with his bag slung in the small of his back, spread his
palms in front of him.

'Do you...,' he croaked, found his voice. 'I say, do you speak English?'

The guard was pointing a Thompson sub-machine gun at him. Robin's skin rebelled, shrank over his stomach at the appalling threat.

'Ben Ingliz,' he called. 'I want to see Genghiz bey.'

Behind him, some way behind him, twenty men slid through shrubberies and trees and there was not a snap of a twig or a clink from the tools of death they carried.

'I am a journalist. Ingliz journalist. I want to see Genghiz.'

It had to work. Before they killed him they had to find out how he knew who they were. They would not risk killing him without knowing. They had to bring him nearer the house.

Claire—there she was, and her father and Donna—behind the glass peering across the gravel and shadows towards him. She must get down. Mundham must realize he must get her on the floor, why doesn't he...?

'Gel. Shimde. Shimde.'

'Come'—that's what it meant—'come'. Or was it 'go'? It had to mean 'come'.

Robin moved forward and let the bag swing to his side, under his arm. The guard was coming to meet him, but the other had turned to watch the prisoners. With perfect coolness Mundham turned away and sat down on the window seat, willing the girls to act with just such a lack of concern. The second guard began to follow the first. Twenty yards, ten. They stopped, eyeing him. Soon they would be dead. Boys. Like his students, but tougher, harder.

He stepped forward boldly.

'I have papers for Genghiz bey,' he said, and his hand slipped into the bag. There was the click of a safety catch thumbed off and the gun levelled at him again. Five yards.

'You must show them to Genghiz then,' said the guard in English.

And at last he allowed Robin to draw level with him, the second guard joined them, they were in line, no longer covering him. His hand came up grasping the canister, fingers squeezing the release valve and the two guards took the full blast of the CS gas in their faces as Robin hurled himself away and behind them.

A red flare shot upwards but before it could reach the height of the trees the air exploded.

From the east Nur, Alp and Dealer could see little of what was happening. The air and the ground beneath them shook with the rapid concussions; they saw the lightning trail of small missiles and felt rather than saw the explosions that were tearing the main part of the villa to pieces with eruptions from the inside. The glass roof of the gazebo shattered and fell in a shower of light and the wooden fabric of the villa was torn into fragments and splinters by bullets and tracer shells, and black smoke began to billow round—in places it seemed almost to be pumped into the dusky air, and orange flames flickered. Nur's stop-watch touched twenty and a sort of silence fell on their bruised ears.

But there was still noise enough. Through the trees to their right the marines came firing from the hip, filtering from cover to cover towards the house. Although no signal had been given Nur began to move forward—at first a steady walk, then, driven by his concern for the hostages and Robin, he broke into a trot. Dealer followed him reluctantly and Alp wheezed and stumbled behind.

The first soldier reached Robin ahead of them. Nur felt relief as the thin tall Englishman struggled to his feet—he looked dazed but apparently unhurt—and he turned towards the gazebo. Donna was staring across towards him or to his left. Her blouse was torn, there was blood on her face and gold still glinted on her cheek. There was a frosting of shattered glass in her hair and on her shoulders. Something glittered in her hand, a long shard of glass perhaps, but the smoke was thickening and it was difficult to be sure. Nur stumbled towards her, but she was finding her way out on her own. Most of the glass had gone from the walls as well as the roof and either ricochets or some internal movement of the villa had distorted the bars. The girl squeezed through, lost her balance, righted herself, and began to run; then, it was like the swoop of a merlin, she launched herself, not at Nur, but passing across his path. The shard was not a shard but a knife, a dagger. There was a long scream, a banshee howl on her lips, and Nur heard the deeper, strangled cry of fear behind him. Dealer turned to run, stumbled.

Nur was frozen with horror and confusion but the young soldier who had helped Robin had quicker reactions. His automatic rifle clattered and Donna, still yards from her quarry, was caught in a gust of metal, was torn, shattered, and flung to the grass. The knife spun in the air, and flashed red in the flames or a last gleam of sunlight.

Nur's concern was for the living. There was a chance that Claire and her father would now appear and the soldier could take them too as a threat. He sprinted to the wrecked gazebo, trying to keep himself between it and the soldier. He peered over the torn cedar wood, between the bars and the jagged glass, through the stifling smoke. Beneath the window seat he could just make out two shapes, dusty bundles of clothes they seemed, and as he looked Paul Mundham turned his head and slowly the figures wriggled themselves out, pushed gingerly at the flakes of glass, unfolded themselves and stood. Claire and her father were all right. Nur circled the gazebo towards them and an uncontrollable grin spread across his face.

Nur thrust his hand across the partition and Paul's palm closed round it.

Their reunion was cut short. There was a shout behind him, he turned and saw Dealer pointing towards the sea, and a man, tall, in a black beret, broke cover and sprinted, crouched and weaving, across the parched lawns towards the boathouses. Genghiz had already covered about fifty yards behind the angle of the villa and there was no one but Nur and Dealer with a clear line of fire until he was almost at the water's edge, where he was seen by the soldiers approaching from the west. A flurry of bullets did indeed splinter the lintel of the doorway above his head as he wrenched it open, possibly he was hit—he seemed to stagger, but within seconds of his appearance he had gone.

Nur and Dealer pounded after him, but as they reached the boathouse, they heard, through all the confused din, the roar of a powerful engine, and a bright orange dart of a speedboat surged out over the dark Marmora, cutting a clear scar of white foam in a shallow arc that curved towards the mouth of the Bosporus.

The boathouse was dark, lit only by the triangle of sea and twilight sky. Nur made out two slipways divided by a stone jetty. The water to one side was still rocking viciously in the wake of the speedboat and a noxious cloud of exhaust fumes swirled above it; on the other side a large inflatable with a heavy outboard engine nudged the stone in time to the lap of the wavelets.

Dealer's feet slapped the wooden bottom.

'We must get after him,' he shouted.

Dealer was trying to slip the painter from its bollard.

'Not fast enough; this maybe is. For Christ's sake, come on.'

Nur dropped in, but felt helpless—more so because he sensed the insane passion in the American's voice.

'Can you work this engine? I can't.'

A third figure appeared in the doorway behind them.
'I can.'

Without further words Paul Mundham joined them in the boat. He wrenched at the starting lanyard, the motor kicked, coughed and roared. He grabbed the tiller, twisted the throttle, and with Nur and Dealer crouched in front of him, the inflatable shot forward.

Far behind them Robin comforted Claire, weeping over the torn body of Donna Liss.

CHAPTER VI

For two summers Paul Mundham had had a lot of pleasure
from his own smaller craft. Uninflated it could be carried
on the roof rack of his car with the outboard motor stowed
in the trunk. At weekends in the summer he would drive
the five miles up to the Thames to potter about the fascinat-
ing reaches of Greenwich and Woolwich or he would go
further down the Kentish coast to Margate, Chatham and
the Isle of Sheppey. His wife had found the boat uncom-
fortable but his son and granchildren loved it and Claire
sometimes came too with her sketch-pad, if he was going
somewhere really interesting and promised to stay in the
same place long enough for her to draw.

But this boat was different—not much bigger, but the
engine at least twice as powerful. There was little or no
sea running yet they hit the first wave with a smack that
bounced the rounded bow high in the air, and then the
bumps came with the volume and regularity of a machine,
spray curved up on either side, occasionally bucketfuls of
sea smashed across them, and the air at forty miles an
hour tore tears from their eyes and dragged their soaked
clothing across their bodies.

Genghiz led by half a minute, say something between a
quarter and a half mile. Paul could not see him but had
noted his direction—to the west and north. Towards the
Bosporus, but the bay was littered with small craft which
were clustering on the villa, drawn by the sounds of battle
and the column of black smoke that now rose above it.

Paul had to concentrate entirely on avoiding collision: throwing the inflatable from side to side, with both hands clenched on the tiller, he was forced into a bent standing position to see over the rearing bow and then thrown forward with a jerk that threatened to loose his grip as they smashed into the troughs. But they were clear of the sightseers quickly—there were fewer of them than he had first supposed—and then he saw him, was sure he had, the flash of orange carving a white 'V' in the black sea ahead.

'I can see him,' he bellowed through the roar of the engine and though the rush of the wind plucked the words away Nur heard him and understood. The Turk hauled himself upright on the rope laced along the rubber side, looked and turned his head back with a grin penetrating the pallor of his drawn streaming face. Dealer did not budge—he was rigid across the flat bottom, both hands fastened on the rope, feet braced against the other side, eyes mostly staring but squeezed tight when the boat swerved particularly viciously.

The orange tipped arrow was gone—hidden by the headland of Moda.

As they raced up to the headland, a point entirely built up with modern blocks, many already lit against the twilit sky, the sea became more menacing—they were feeling the first of the current from the Bosporus and the stiff cold breeze blowing above it from the Black Sea. The boat began to buck and kick yet more violently with spine-jarring thuds and, in those uncertain waters, it swung from side to side in what would have been roll in a keeled boat. Yet ahead, and as far as he could tell no further ahead than before, there again was their quarry, shooting beneath the stem of one of the giant ships that lay at anchor across the roads, a tanker, Russian, Paul somehow noticed as they came up with it, about half a mile off the long breakwater protecting Haydarpasha.

And now the sea became less vicious as they came into the Bosporus and left the Marmora—still choppy, but evenly so—a swift steady current that could be handled, at least while Genghiz allowed them to keep to the middle, away from the eddies near the banks. Paul saw him clearly again leaving Leander's Tower well to the starboard before taking the first bend round Scutari and out of sight again. Ahead of him, beyond the rock with its square lighthouse tower, the Dolmabahce Palace lay, already floodlit, a long slab of iced cake beneath the Hilton; to his left the older palaces, the domes and towers of Topkapi struck up black against the lilac sky; and above swirled the endless spirals the clouds of migrant storks already bewildered between dying thermals and the menace of the narrow strait.

There was more shipping to deal with: the ferries, caïques, laden barges, and a sea-going yacht with graceful lines chugging home to one of the expensive marinas after a day of deep-sea fishing for swordfish in the Marmora; then a long straight stretch of three miles and Genghiz clearly in view, his lead a little longer but the whiteness of his wake more plain than before on the darkening water, still going like a bat out of hell. The banks close in a little here, the narrowest part of all. Genghiz seemed nearer now as he fought the faster current first but then the gain was lost—the inflatable had a greater surface area in or on the water and was certainly less streamlined, and to Mundham it was almost as if the water was tacky, sticking to the flat bottom, threatening to drag them back. But they were in no danger of losing Genghiz, not for five or ten minutes anyway, provided they hit nothing and the fuel held out.

Provided they hit nothing ... Paul could not help becoming aware that he was suffering: cramps had seized hold of his limbs, his chest ached with a deep throbbing pain, his fingers were numb and he felt terrified that he would lose control of them, his vision was blurred, confused by whirling spots and sparks of purple and green in the retina of his eyes, and the splash of white ahead divided and mixed as he strove to focus on it. He sought relief, for his eyes at any rate, to port and starboard. They had left the City: small suburbs with little harbours tricked out in fairy lights, old wooden villas often rising sheer from the water, trees, and another palace small and graceful—a piece of Venice set down in a park—all slid by. A flock of shearwaters, lost souls of the dead the Istanbulis call them, skimmed along the wavelets. It was getting dark quickly now, perhaps it would soon be dark enough for Genghiz to cut his engine and his tell-tale wake, slip into a harbour amongst the yachts, and lose himself on land before they could be sure of where he had gone.

'Look, he's going in.'

Paul hardly caught the shouted words, but the meaning of Nur's outflung arm was unmistakeable, and, yes, the orange speedboat had left the middle, was sweeping in towards the eastern shore, towards a small piece of Asia that jutted out into the stream a mile or so south of Rumeli Hisar, the huge castle built by the Conqueror which dominates the strait at its narrowest point. Genghiz was nearer and nearer the shore—he must, thought Paul, be thinking of landing, he must land, prayed Paul aware of nothing but the fact that he could not, it was impossible, hold on for any longer.

The white wake blossomed—momentarily they caught a glimpse of the whole orange hull as it spun in a tight half circle—then died as the speedboat cut back to quarter throttle then nothing. They saw Genghiz leap from his still moving boat on to a low quay. He clutched for a bollard, hesitated swaying on the very edge, and then, balance regained, disappeared into the gloom.

They had gained—perhaps in the dusk Genghiz had not been sure of his landing. The rubber bow bounced on the quay less than thirty seconds behind the speedboat which, propelled by Genghiz's kick for the shore, was already drifting slowly away on the current. Paul held the inflatable against the quay with the motor just ticking over as Nur then Dealer clambered unsteadily on to land, Dealer obscenely cursing cold cramped limbs that would not do as he wanted. As the American sprawled by the bollard a shot rang out from the gloom ahead; Nur dropped to one knee and Paul saw the flashes from his outflung hands as the policeman's service revolver returned fire. The reports were like slaps round his aching ears. Trying to keep his head down he edged forward searching the flat floor for the painter. He found it, cut the engine, stumbled forward and grasped the bollard. Sickeningly the boat pushed outwards under his feet and he had not the strength to resist the drag. A strong hand found his armpit and he was hauled on to the stone flags where he lay completely flat, not because he feared more shooting, but because he was quite unable to do anything else.

'Are you all right?' Nur spoke urgently.

Paul could only gasp and grunt.

'Look, stay here. Someone will come soon. You'll be all right.' There was a real note of anxiety—Nur was torn between leaving the Englishman unprotected where there were probably more of Genghiz's men about, and losing valuable seconds.

Distantly a car door slammed and Dealer, quite close, shouted.

'He's got a car, round the front, on the road.'

Paul lifted his head, and, as if he were putting himself together by stages, managed with Nur's help to get to his feet. He saw that they were on a narrow terrace between road and sea, a terrace littered with metal tables and chairs. To his left there was a low building with a trellised veranda, overgrown with vines and some other creeper, with the words painted in black on the white stucco and still legible in the fading light, 'Saray Lokantisi'. A café, a bit seedy, apparently deserted. A car starter drummed hoarsely from somewhere out of sight and stopped, drummed again; the engine coughed and died.

'For Christ's sake—move,' bellowed Dealer, but he wouldn't move on his own, even though, as Mundham now noticed, he too had a gun.

Nur gave Mundham's shoulder a firm pat which had a touch of decision and authority in it and he and Dealer began to push briskly through the tables towards the corner of the café. Paul hesitated and realized he still had the painter in his hand. He looped it carefully over the bollard and then, cautiously, set out after them. He was surprised to find that he could walk though he cannoned from table to table and knocked two over.

The engine fired and roared, there was the tortured scream of crashed gears, the jolting revving of a car whose driver has not mastered the pedals, then it roared again just as Dealer reached the road. The American fired once, but the car was already on its way.

Nur barked into his miniaturized radio, while Dealer cursed and Paul sank with relief into a still upright chair. Paul realized his breath was almost normal and that the pain was ebbing leaving a sick watery weakness in his joints. He looked around. There was still no sign of life from the café. The windows were shuttered, a door fastened with a bar. Closed for the night or the season. A pleasure cruiser, all lit up, music playing, glided by on the current, heading back for the City. A lorry thundered past, empty crates swaying; then, at last, the wail of a police siren.

It was a 'Trafik Patrol' car, boldly painted in black and white, manned by two uniformed policemen, and a blue beacon circled flashes of urgent light from its roof. They were in almost before it had stopped, the three men clawing at the upholstery, almost fighting each other for a place on the wide back seat as the lurch of the accelerating car pushed them back on top of each other. Nur shouted orders; the driver, grim and curt, answered crisply without looking back. Street lamps and houses flashed by and the siren howled around them.

'You've lost him. You have fucking lost him.'

To Paul's right Dealer banged the top of the front seat with his fist. His face was swollen and dark crimson. On Paul's left Nur leant over the driver's shoulder, his eyes hooded and hawk-like searching the road in front.

'I don't think so.'

'For Christ's sake he's got five minutes on us.'

'Not more than three. If he heads north he'll meet road blocks. But I think he will have turned east about a kilometre up the road. If he picked up the Botulin XP3 at that café, that's what he will have done.'

Paul's curiosity was stirred. 'Why?' he asked.

'The Fresh Waters of Asia. About eight kilometres up in the hills. A "barrage"—what do you call it? A dam.'

A reservoir, of course.

The road, a black ribbon, wound in beneath their wheels. Paul could not keep his eyes on it. He sank back, and remembering the wartime trick of dozing when he could, felt his body relax away in the sudden warmth of the car. Uncontrolled images flooded upon his mind—images of nightmare and soul searing anxiety. He remembered the helicopter to Siirt and the long journey back and the agony of being near Claire but always out of sight. He remembered the loneliness of the Park Hotel and the horror of the policeman—what was his name? Gökalp—gunned down by the waterside. Then the relentless cross-examination, the humiliation of a thorough body search, and then yet more questioning from Genghiz, the madman carrying his load of destruction to the Fresh Waters of Asia in front of them. Then the gazebo, the wait through the long day, and Bury, at last, strolling down the drive towards them.

But that was all right. It was all right. He had seen Bury—Robin—and Claire in each other's arms, before he had remembered the inflatable and set out after Nur and Dealer on this terrifying absurd pursuit. But they were all right. They had been pleased to see each other. He rather thought they might marry. He hoped they would. (He chuckled quietly and Nur glanced at him, at the heavy solid Englishman who was still with them, and who shouldn't be, who should be safe in bed with his daughter safely near him. But Mundham was all right— he looked sane, almost contented.) Paul was thinking it was about time someone else, a bit younger, a bit fitter, undertook to look after this wayward daughter—he was too old for another escapade of this sort.

His mind drifted back a couple of years. He remembered an endless weekend in Barcelona, the offices shut, the lawyers and police in their tidy apartments while Claire sat out two more days in jail, possibly a month pregnant and facing a charge that could leave her in jail for another six years. That had been as bad as this. At five o'clock on the Sunday he had gone to the bullfight, and lonely, cold sober, had seen six bulls, defiant and proud, reduced to bewilderment, and then weakness, and then death. Yet there had been something in the spectacle, a sort of beauty, a sort of knowledge...

'How much further?' Dealer on his right.

'Three kilometres. Not more.'

Paul came to with a start. They were racing up a hill-side road, deserted, now almost dark though the sky still glowed in the West with something more than starlight. Giant trees, a rich forest of them, were closing round and the car's slipstream roared with the closeness of them. The siren had stopped, Paul could not say when. Dealer moved and metal clicked, a smell of oil and cordite with it. He was cleaning and loading his gun, muttering to himself as he worked. There was a stale smell of acrid sweat about him, fear perhaps, that Paul did not like, and, strangely, he remembered the second bull, the one that had died badly with gobbets of blood splashing over its lolling tongue on to the sand.

'This is it.'

Above the trees a long high curved wall hung with a chain of lamps appeared; the trees thinned and the parabolic curve of the dam towered above them dwarfing the group of low buildings and the car parked in front of them. There were lights everywhere, dazzling after the darkness of the road.

'He's here. The car's here.'

And two bodies huddled near it, bleeding on to the asphalt—a nightwatchman and an engineer, one in the doorway of the nearest building, the nightwatchman near the car with his whistle still clamped absurdly between his teeth.

They all spilled out, hugging the shelter of the car and crouched to the ground, the dry dust pricking their nostrils, and the electric hum of the dynamos in their ears. Mundham peered round. Two lines of light climbed the hillside on both sides of the gleaming white wall, marking footpaths to the top, to the reservoir—millions of gallons, of tons of water held above them in concrete chains.

'He can't be far up yet,' muttered Dealer. 'That case is heavy.'

An automatic rifle clattered above them in answer and the bullets tore the asphalt around them; one clanged on the wing of the car and whined away.

Nur spoke, first in Turkish, then in English.

'He's up on the right hand track. Two thirds of the way up. I, Dealer and the driver will break for it and get after him. Mr Mundham you will stay here with the other policeman. He must go on climbing, we should reach cover before he can drop the case and shoot again. Now.'

But only two broke from the cover of the car—first Nur, then the driver. Sixty yards to some sort of cover, sixty yards of bare well-lit asphalt. Paul watched, curled round the rear tyres of the car, his gorge rising on an agony of anxiety: forty, thirty, twenty yards eaten back by the policemen's pounding feet and the horror as the air exploded above them again and the driver was plucked off his course, his body torn and twisted, hurled through the air to crumple on the ground within yards of the shadow. He did not lie still: he writhed, screamed and then, retched out a reluctant life. But Nur was through. His revolver cracked again and again, drawing Genghiz's fire, the cape to draw off the bull from the gored picador.

A hoarse whisper snarled round Paul's head.

'Good, good. He'll never get him now. Not without covering fire.'

Paul could not believe his ears.

'You want Genghiz to tip that muck in the reservoir?'

'For Christ's sake, yes. That's been the whole point: get the guerrillas to poison the water supplies, spread plague, Russian plague, and catch them at it. It'll set them back years and years. But that fool policeman would never see it...'

More shots rang out, the flashes higher up on the hillside, perhaps only forty feet from the curving parapet. Paul edged further behind the car, his eyes wide and helpless, searching for some possibility.... Dealer chuckled again.

'Stupid with it. He should never have followed Genghiz. He could have gone up the other side as fast as he liked with no chance of being pinned down. Now Genghiz can take his time and pick him off when he likes...' the machine gun rattled again, '... if he hasn't got him already.'

In an alchemy of passion Paul's frustration turned to

rage and he swung round awkwardly with clenched fist. His weight was behind the blow and it smacked Dealer's head against the corner of the rear fender with considerable force. To his amazement the American subsided—dazed, stunned, perhaps unconscious. Paul crouched, pulled in a huge mouthful of cordite-tainted air and then loosed himself across the car-park for the path on the opposite side to Nur's. Every step jarred his tortured body, almost immediately the pains blossomed like Roman candles in his chest, all the way he expected his body to be shredded like the driver's but he made it, stumbling and retching into a shrubbery at the foot of the hill, only yards from where the small street lamp marked the foot of the left hand path.

Gasping and clutching his side he glanced back. They were shooting again a hundred or more yards away on the other side, but not at him, nor at the car. There was just a chance that he had got across unseen, at least by Genghiz. He dragged himself beyond the lamp; above him the path, marked by largish whitewashed stones snaked through bushes and round rocks, vanishing as it hair-pinned up the steep slope. He hauled himself upright and forced himself into a laboured run.

The pitch of the path was an insult, then a torment, and finally an absurdity. Do what he could with them his legs refused to accelerate: they began to ache like columns of flaccid, hot lead. Insanely he remembered the underground, Piccadilly Circus and late for an appointment, the escalators packed and how, quite recently, he had tried to race up the central stairs. At the top he had vowed to take taxis for the rest of his life, but there were no taxis here. At least the path was well-surfaced with some sort of non-slip composite, but it twisted so, and every lamp with its pool of light was a terror and surely Genghiz would hear the roar of his breath. The path had become an Eiger, every yard to be clawed down to him by his mutinous feet, yet he was climbing, he was climbing. Already the car park was a ring of light below him, and the dam had curved into an almost sheer white wall only yards away on his right. Then something stirred by the patrol car, an inky blob stirred from the hard straight edge of shadow, and he realized Dealer was moving. Fear of the madman below, behind him, as well as of the madman above him, turned him and drove him on up.

Then the miracle happened. The path flattened, circled a large boulder and spread itself into a little plateau and beyond stretched the long curve of the dam, topped with a railed cat-walk, perhaps a couple of yards wide. On one side a vast expanse of black water, on the other the long, dry drop down to the sluices and dynamos, the sheds and the car park, a hundred feet or more below.

As he gazed across it from the shadows which he instinctively clung to, a figure broke loose at the far end, maybe a hundred and fifty yards away. It was Genghiz, clear enough, but exposed, completely vulnerable in the lights. For a heart-wrenching second Paul was convinced that Nur must be dead, for why else did he not shoot the gangster down? Then he saw why not. The gangster was backing slowly along the spare beauty of the parapet with the case of plague held balanced on the rail by his left hand, while his right cradled the automatic rifle at his hip. Paul heard him calling, a taunting defiance in his voice, and then more distantly Nur's reply, commanding, demanding, pleading. Paul could not understand a word, but the situation was clear enough. If Nur fired the case and its abominable contents would topple into the water, and Paul had no doubt the phials were already smashed, the white crystals free to absorb the Fresh Waters and melt into them.

Yet he could not see what Genghiz hoped to achieve. For the moment the guerrilla held the life of the city beneath the palm of his hand, but it could not save him.

Only there, totally exposed, was he a danger. As soon as he reached the other end of the dam, Paul's end, the threat would cease to exist, and he could be hunted down. And even now police sirens wailed far down the valley below.

Paul had faced Genghiz the night before. The dark eyes had flashed and stared at him across a table in the villa, but as the hours ticked by he had forgotten the eyes and saw only the teeth, bared white between thin, withdrawn lips, and the questions had become fewer and their place, as Genghiz's hold on his purpose had weakened, had been taken by invective, slogans, and finally the hate-filled, destructive paranoia of an arrogant madman. Paul now realized that Genghiz was not holding the case of Botulin XP3 over the water as a threat or a bargaining counter, but, trapped at last, was waiting for the audience he needed before tipping it over the edge. No doubt he would be gunned down but he would take a city with him and Dealer would gain just the outcome he wanted.

Casting about, Paul found at the margin of the path a white-washed rock. He hefted it up and judged it to be about ten pounds in weight. He put it by him and pulled off his shoes and socks. His feet, white, skinny, blotched with veins, an old man's feet, looked peculiarly stupid, and what he was going to do was stupid too, but perhaps just possible. He picked up the rock, and began to pad noiselessly towards the madman's back, and as he did, the madman edged slowly backwards towards him, towards the middle of the dam: Genghiz would go from the centre, a gesture like his demanded that.

Paul walked quite briskly, the stone held high. Below, the sirens wailed louder, yet in spite of them he could hear Nur talking more urgently and Paul knew that he had been seen, that Nur was striving to hold the madman's attention. As the Englishman tracked along the great shallow arc he began to feel light-headed, almost exalted. There was a cool breeze and it began to ruffle his sparse hair, and he found he could control his breathing. There was more noise, he realized, than he had been aware of: the steady drumming of thousands of gallons of water far beneath their feet, the hum of dynamos, the distraction of the approaching cars, it really did seem he would do it. Twenty paces, fifteen, ten. Surely Genghiz would sense him, by vibration, by disturbance of the air, by body temperature if nothing else, surely anyone would sense someone so close behind...

'Mundham...'

The shout seemed horrifyingly close, but Paul's purpose did not slacken for more than a tenth of a second. He lunged forward and the rock in his left hand circled down from above his shoulder smashing into the skull behind the ear, and Genghiz was swung by the blow downwards and to the side and his collapsing weight tipped the case inwards away from the water. Paul swung again, this time from below, caught the shoulder this time, seemed to lift the tall man into the rail which acted like a fulcrum and toppled him over. The body plummeted, smacked the outward curve of the dam, somersaulted, bounced away and slid like a bundle of broken sticks, down the long, long slope.

Paul crouched over the black case, clutching it, cradling it, and turned to face Dealer who had shouted his name from behind him.

The American came stumbling along the cat-walk, his huge hands grabbing and hauling the rails on either side of him. His boot caught Mundham in the stomach, lifted him back hopelessly winded, and the case was now free again between them. Dealer hung over it, panting, his face distorted; then he relaxed, he uncurled his body and stood astride the case. A grin split his bovine features.

'You crazy, no good, mother-loving, limey bastard. Christ, won't you ever learn?'

And with an effort, for the case was strongly made and

heavy, he began to shift it with his foot towards the darkness of the water lapping only a few feet below.

There was one shot. The top of his head seemed to burst open and he went down instantly like the second bull that had received the 'descabello' in the Barcelona bull-ring.

Colonel Nur came up behind Paul. His face was dead white, marked by the black clefts that had once been the lines on the face of a prematurely ageing man. He was shaking so much he could not return his revolver to its holster beneath his jacket.

'They were mad.'

There was no plea or excuse in his voice, only the finality of deep despair. 'They were both mad. And all the others like them.'

The car park below had filled with vehicles and as Nur and Paul gazed down the engines and sirens died. Men spilled out and then hesitated, gazing upwards. One or two began to run to the paths but most of them seemed small, rather lost, as if doubtful of what to do.

And then Paul heard the purposeful beat of huge wings and saw, flighted in 'V' formation, and heading east out of the very last dying embers of the day, a flock of large birds. The storks, at least, seemed to know where they were going.